Two

Betrothed
Edo and Enam

The **Toby Press S.Y. Agnon Library**
Jeffrey Saks, Series Editor

Books from this series

A Book That Was Lost: Thirty-Five Stories

To This Day

Shira

A Simple Story

*Two Scholars That Were in Our Town
and Other Novellas*

Two Tales: Betrothed & Edo and Enam

The Book of State: Agnon's Political Satires (forthcoming)

A Guest for the Night (forthcoming)

The Bridal Canopy (forthcoming)

And the Crooked Shall be Made Straight (forthcoming)

In Mr. Lublin's Store (forthcoming)

*Forevermore & Other Stories of the
Old World and the New (forthcoming)*

Illustrated:
From Foe to Friend & Other Stories by S.Y. Agnon
A Graphic Novel by Shay Charka

TWO TALES

BETROTHED ❧ EDO AND ENAM

S.Y. AGNON

TRANSLATED FROM THE HEBREW BY
WALTER LEVER

NEWLY REVISED AND ANNOTATED BY
JEFFREY SAKS

WITH AN AFTERWORD BY
ROBERT ALTER

The Toby Press

Two Tales
by S.Y. Agnon
Translated by Walter Lever
Revised and Annotated by Jeffrey Saks
© 2014 *The* Toby Press LLC

These two stories are available in Agnon's Hebrew volume
'Ad Henah, part of the Collected Writings of S.Y. Agnon –
Kol Sippurav shel Shmuel Yosef Agnon, © Schocken Publishing House Ltd
(Jerusalem and Tel Aviv), most recent edition 1998.

First English Edition © 1966
Published by arrangement with Schocken Publishing House Ltd,
an imprint of The Knopf Doubleday Publishing
Group, a division of Random House, Inc.

Unless otherwise noted, images accompanying annotations
appear under Creative Commons License, CC-BY 2.0

The Toby Press LLC
POB 8531, New Milford, CT 06776–8531, USA
& POB 2455, London W1A 5WY, England
www.tobypress.com

ISBN 978-1-59264-356-1

Typeset in Garamond by Koren Publishing Services

Printed and bound in the United States

Contents

Preface

As we near the fiftieth anniversary of the awarding of the Nobel Prize in Literature to S.Y. Agnon, Toby Press is pleased to issue this revised and newly annotated edition of *Two Tales*, which, when published in 1966 – the year he received the prize – was the first sampling of his "modern" stories made available in English.

Although the product of the same period of creativity, the conjoining of the two stories in one stand-alone volume was a conceit of the English-language edition (in Hebrew they appear as part of a much larger collection, *'Ad Henah*). Nevertheless, the two stories are clearly in dialogue with one another, sharing elements of moonstruck sleepwalkers, disengaged academics, and the typically Agnonian unfulfilled love. On the other hand, the divergent tones of the two stories are remarkable when read side by side: "Betrothed" is set in a world of familiar reality (albeit with the intrusion of a surreal and indeterminate conclusion); "Edo and Enam" projects a dreamlike unreality, infused with mystery and mysticism, from beginning to end.

"**Betrothed**" (the story's title is more properly translated as "Betrothal Oath"; a promise to marry) was first published in 1943, and quickly became the subject of significant scholarly and critical debate. A childhood oath between Jacob and Shoshana, sworn at the edge of a Viennese garden pool (recall Biblical Jacob and Rachel's well, Genesis 29), is reintroduced with force in their adult lives when they are reunited in Jaffa at the story's outset. Set in pre-World War I Palestine, it is this reunion, after many years, and its conjuring of memories of childhood promises and pains, which drives the plot.

Among the revisions to this edition is calling our heroine by her given name, Shoshanah. In the original translation, she had inexplicably been christened "Susan" – perhaps "Shoshanah" was considered too ethnic a name for mid-century American readers. This revision to the translation will hopefully allow the reader to sense some of the symbolism and word-play at work – Shoshanah meaning "rose" in Agnon's most botanical of tales should not be a fact the reader can be allowed to overlook. (The precise meaning of "Shoshanah", alternatively lily or rose depending on the layer of Hebrew one is speaking, is less important than the floral echo lent to the story.) Those familiar with Jewish liturgy will recall the line of the Purim song *"Shoshanat Ya'akov tzahalah ve-samehah"* – *"Jacob's rose rejoiced and was glad"* – that is "The joining of Jacob and Shoshanah was a source for rejoicing and gladness" highlights the bitterness of the fact that, as Gershon Shaked has pointed out, the union of Jacob and Shoshanah does *not* seem to foster such joy. Or, as Dina Stern suggests in her unraveling of the story's subterranean sources (or, in "Betrothed", submarinal) – Shoshanah Ehrlich is the tragic incarnation of the heroine of Song of Songs: "My beloved has gone down to his garden, to the spice beds, to graze in the gardens and to gather roses. I am my beloved's, and my beloved is mine, who grazes among the roses" (6:2–3).

Dov Sadan pointed to "Betrothed" as proof that even Agnon's stories that do not appear puzzling or enigmatic or deeply allegorical on the surface can still be interpreted as rich allegories – in fact they almost demand it. Nevertheless, the narrative accomplishment allows the work to function on the "revealed" level of surface reading (*peshat*, in the language of Biblical interpretation) while hiding a complex allegory underneath. Not for nothing did Shaked compare "Betrothed" to Oedipus, Sleeping Beauty, Hamsun's Scandanavian provincial novels, and Roth's *Portnoy's Complaint!*

On the other hand, **"Edo and Enam"** (first published in Fall 1950) is a story so enigmatic and seemingly inexplicable that it can hardly sustain a "simple reading" at all. While Arnold Band has inveighed against the unfortunate focus on its complexity, which "distracts the reader and critic from the aesthetic charm of the story," we are still confronted with an exceedingly rich tale; rich in themes, symbols, allusions, and Agnon's intertextualities, with an unusually heavy dose of kabbalistic resonances. (That being said, for the non-Hebrew reader, Band's treatment of the tale is still the best available in English, for its plot summary, review of the criticism that had preceded him, exploration of themes, and overall literary analysis; see Arnold J. Band, *Nostalgia and Nightmare: A Study in the Fiction of S. Y. Agnon*, pp. 382–396.)

In all cases, whether Band is correct about the degree of enigma enveloping "Edo and Enam", we the readers still need to get at the elusive essential meaning of the story, which is set in Jerusalem of the final years of the British Mandate. The nameless narrator is house-sitting for the Greifenbachs, who have left behind their tenant Dr. Ginat, usually engrossed in his philological academic work or away conducting his research on the lost language of Edo and the Enamite Hymns. The itinerant manuscript merchant, Gamzu, is married to an exotic woman Gemulah, whom he had brought back to Jerusalem from her distant home among the lost tribe of Gad, where Ginat's mysterious languages and hymns are still spoken and sung. It is this removal from her source that leads to Gemulah's strange sickness. If it is a reunion that sets the plot of "Betrothed" in motion, here it is severance (of person from place, Gemulah from Gad; person from person, Gemulah from both Ginat and from Gamzu) which drives the events to their tragic end. (Through the good graces of the garrulous game of gutteral *gimmel*-words the reader should have a sense of the alliterative word-play Agnon is up to in this story.) It is the triangle of Gemulah-Ginat-Gamzu which becomes the focus of the tale, most of which is told through narrative conversation. If produced for the stage, the drama would look a lot like a drawing room play, set within Greifenbach's book-lined study. We the audience would hear of the recluse Ginat and then hear the tormented Gamzu tell the tale of Gemulah. But no Noël Coward play would this be! There is nothing droll going on in Greifenbach's drawing room, aside perhaps from

Gerda's speculation that Ginat has magically created a women for himself up in his room. More than she could know, that, too, turns out to be more tragic than comedic, as the final scene shifts out of the drawing room and up to the rooftop.

Baruch Kurzweil identified connections between "Edo and Enam" and Agnon's *Sefer HaMa'asim* story cycle, and its dreamlike or nightmarish surrealism. If "Betrothed" can be read as Agnon's modern midrash on Song of Songs, Kurzweil is correct in identifying "Edo and Enam" as his take on Ecclesiastes – with its focus on themes of eros and death.

Finally, when we describe these *Two Tales* as exemplars of Agnon's modern stories, we mean set in the "new world" of revived Jewish life in the Land of Israel, not the *Yishuv HaYashan* of Jerusalem of old, nor Galicia of Reb Yudel in *The Bridal Canopy*. But they are modern in a more essential way as well. In the end, Jacob, like so many of the Jews of the Second *Aliya*, departs for America; Gemulah – in a story that portrays tensions between source and destiny (Meshulam Tochner's hermeneutical explanation of the title) cannot survive in the new Jerusalem when taken out of her native element. These stories, authored shortly before and immediately after the establishment of the State of Israel, raise very "modern" questions about Jewish life, and like so much of Agnon's writing, explore the connection and disconnection between "what was and what is", "tradition and modernity", "there and here" – and the degree to which the two sides of each of these dyads can be bridged, if at all.

Jeffrey Saks
Editor, The S.Y. Agnon Library
The Toby Press
Tisha B'Av 5774 (Agnon's 126th birthday)

Betrothed

Jaffa view from Hôtel du Parc.

I

JAFFA IS THE DARLING OF THE WATERS: THE WAVES of the Great Sea kiss her shores, a blue sky is her daily cover, she brims with every kind of people, Jews and Ishmaelites and Christians, busy at trade, at shipping and labor. But there are others in Jaffa who take no part in any of these: teachers, for instance, and such a one was Jacob Rechnitz, something of whose story we are about to tell.

When Jacob Rechnitz had completed his term of study and been crowned with a doctorate, he joined a group of travelers going up to the Holy Land. He saw the land and it was good, and those that dwelt within it, they were tranquil and serene. And he said to himself, If only I could earn my bread here, I should settle in this land. Jaffa was his dearest love, for she lay at the lips of the sea, and Rechnitz had always devoted himself to all that grows in the sea. He happened to visit a school, and that school needed a teacher of Latin and German. The authorities saw him, deliberated on him; they offered him a post as teacher, and he accepted.

Now Rechnitz was a botanist by profession and expert in the natural sciences. But as the natural sciences were already in the hands of another teacher, while the post of Latin and German was vacant, it was this post that was assigned him. For sometimes it is not the position that makes the man, but the man who makes the position, though it must also be said that Rechnitz was a suitable choice.

So Rechnitz set to work. He met his duties faithfully. He chose the right books and did not weigh his students down with tedious topics. He was never bitter with his students; never too proud with his fellow teachers, most of whom were self-taught. His students loved him, his colleagues accepted him. His students, because he treated them as friends; his colleagues, because he allowed them to treat *him* as one. And, too, his tall bearing and deep voice, his manners and his chestnut eyes that looked with affection on everyone, gained him the love of all. Not more than a month or two had passed before he had won a good name in the town. Not more than a month or two before he had become a favorite guest of fathers whose daughters had come to know him before the fathers themselves.

The fever of land speculation had already passed. The money-chasers, who had sought to profit from the soil of Israel, had gone bankrupt and cleared out. Jaffa now belonged to those who knew that this land is unlike all others; she yields herself only to those honest workers who labor with her. Some engaged in trade and some in the skills of which the land had need; others lived on the funds they had brought from abroad. Nor one nor the other asked too much of life. They left the Turk to his seat of power and sought protection in the shade of the foreign consulates, which looked on them more kindly than had the lands of their birth. The dreamers awoke from their dreams, and men of deeds began to dream dreams of a spiritual center and a land of Israel belonging to Israel. From time to time they would gather and argue about the country and its community, and send reports of their proceedings to the Council of the Lovers of Zion in Odessa. And all the while, each man was father to his sons and daughters, and husband to his wife, and friend to his friends.

Life was unexacting, very little happened. The days slipped by quietly, people were undemanding. Their needs were limited and easily satisfied. The well-to-do were content to live in small dwellings, to wear simple clothes and to eat modestly. A man would rise early in the morning, drink his glass of tea and take a few olives or some vegetables with his bread, work until lunch time and come home before dusk. By then the samovar was steaming, neighbors paid calls, tea and preserves were handed round. If some learned man were present, he would make fun of the hotel-keeper who had misunderstood a Talmudic word, and called fruit preserves "jam." Or if a farmer were in the company, his conversation would be about the uprooting of vines and the planting of almonds, about officials and bribes. Or if a visitor from Jerusalem happened to be there, he would tell them what was going on in the City: if he were a cheerful type, he might amuse the company with a Jerusalem joke. If there were only local Jaffa folk present, they would discuss the news from abroad, even though it was already stale by the time the foreign newspapers arrived.

Jacob Rechnitz was welcome and warmly received in every house. He appreciated people's efforts to speak German for his benefit, and pleased them in return with the smattering of Russian he had picked up. (Russian and Yiddish were still used rather than Hebrew; as for Rechnitz, he came from central Europe, where German was the common tongue.) Like most bachelors, he was glad to be brought into company; he fell in with his hosts' ways of thinking so completely that it seemed to him that their views were indeed his own. Every now and then he would be invited to an evening meal; and afterwards, when the head of the family settled down to reading the latest journal, whether it was *Hashilo'ah* in Hebrew or *Razsvyet* in Russian, he would take a stroll with the daughters of the house. There was always light for such walks: if there were no moon, the stars would be shining; and if there were no stars, the girls' eyes did well enough. Another young man would ask for no more than such a life; but as for Rechnitz, another world lay in his heart: love of the sea and of research into her plants. Even at the season when Jaffa's hot air saps the marrow and the spirit of most men, he remained vigorous. From this same sea that brought profit to shipowners, carried vessels weighted with wares for merchants and yielded up fish for the fishermen; from these waters, Jacob Rechnitz drew forth his plants. Under the sea's surface he had already discovered certain kinds of vegetation that no scientist had ever seen. He had written about them to his professor; and his professor, glad to have a capable scholar stationed in such a region, had published his reports in the Vienna periodical brought out by the Imperial and Royal Society for Botanical and Zoological Studies. Besides this, he urged his favorite pupil to persevere in his research, since no investigation into the marine plants off that coast had been undertaken so far.

Rechnitz needed no urging. He belonged to the sea as a bay belongs to its shore. Each day he would go out to take whatever the sea offered him; and if the hour was right, he would hire a fishing boat. Yehia, the Yemenite Jew who served as the school's caretaker, would haggle for him with the Arab fishermen; and off he would sail to where, as he told himself, the earliest ancestors of man had had their dwelling. Plying his net and his iron implements, drawing up specimens of seaweed not found along the beach, his heart beat like a hunter's at the chase. Rechnitz was never seasick; no, these mysteries beneath the waters, these marvels of creation, gave him fortitude. There they grew like gardens, like thickets, like shadowed woods among the waters, their appearance varying from the yellow of sulphur to Tyrian purple to flesh tints; they were like clear pearls, like olives, like coral, like a peacock's feathers, clinging to the reefs and the jutting rocks. "My orchard, my vineyard," he would say lovingly. And when he came back from the sea, he would wash his specimens in fresh water, which removes the salt that puffs them out, before laying them in a flat dish. (Anyone watching him might suppose that he was preparing a salad for himself, but he would forget his food for the sake of his plants.) Then he would take them from the dish and spread them out on sheets of thick paper; their slime was enough to make them adhere. Only a few of the world's botanists are concerned with marine plants, and of these few Rechnitz alone was at work on the seaweed off the coast of the Land of Israel, investigating its qualities and means of growth and reproduction. Most scientists can only conduct marine research intermittently, on days when they are free from university duties; but Rechnitz was out every day of the year, in sunshine and rain, by day or by night, when the sea was warmed by the sun and when it was cold, in calm or storm, when other folk slept or when they were busy with their affairs. Had his concern been with the study and classification of plants on dry land, he would have become a celebrity, been made a member of learned societies and spent his time at discussions, meetings and conferences. But since his activities were in a sphere remote from the interests of the Jewish settlement, his name was unknown in the land and his time was his own. He carried on with his investigations and collected many plants. If he found a specimen he could not iden-tify, he would send it abroad, hoping his teachers might know more about it. So it came about that they named a certain seaweed after him, the *Caulerpa Rechnitzia.* It was not long before he was invited to contribute an account of the larger seaweeds for Professor Horst's famous work *Cryptogams of the Mediterranean.*

II

This is how Rechnitz's interest in his field began. When he first entered the university he chose no special subject but applied himself to all the sciences, and particularly the natural sciences, for these had drawn his heart. He already thought of himself as an eternal student, one who would never leave the walls of the academy. But one night he was reading Homer. He heard a voice like the voice of the waves, though he had never yet set eyes on the sea. He shut his book and raised his ears to listen. And the voice exploded, leaping like the sound of many waters. He stood up and looked outside. The moon hung in the middle air, between the clouds and stars; the earth was still. He went back to his book and read. Again he heard the same voice. He put down the book and lay on his bed. The voices died away, but that sea whose call he had heard spread itself out before him, endlessly, while the moon hovered over the face of the waters, cool and sweet and terrible. Next day Rechnitz felt as lost as a man whom the waves have cast up on a desolate island, and so it was for all the days that followed. He began to study less and read books about sea voyages; and all that he read only added to his longing, he might as well have drunk seawater to relieve a thirst. The next step was to cast about for a profession connected with the sea: he took up medicine, with the idea of becoming a ship's doctor. But as soon as he entered the anatomy hall he fainted; he knew then that this could never be his calling. Once, however, Rechnitz happened to visit a friend who was doing research on seaweed. This man, who had just come back from a voyage, showed him the specimens he had brought. Rechnitz saw and was amazed at how much grows in the sea and how little we know about it all. He had scarcely parted from his friend before he realized what he was seeking.

Perhaps this story about Rechnitz reading Homer, with all that followed in its wake, is little more than a legend. But after all it would seem to be less unlikely than other explanations of how he began his career. In any case, when he had finished his studies he left for the Land of Israel; a prize received from the university and a gift bestowed on him by Herr Gotthold Ehrlich defrayed his expenses.

III

This Herr Ehrlich who assisted Jacob Rechnitz on his journey, and who had previously helped him to enter high school, was a wealthy merchant and the honorary consul of a small country which does not take up much space on the map. The garden of his villa adjoined the house of Rechnitz's father, and when Jacob was small he used to play with Shoshanah, the Consul's only daughter. She was a capricious child, who took a special fancy to the boy and would not allow any of the other little girls to join in their games. "Jacob is all mine," she used to say, "and when I'm grown up I am going to marry him." To confirm this, she cut off one of her curls, as well as one of his, and mingled them together. She burned them and they ate the ashes and took a solemn vow to be faithful to each other.

Jacob was treated kindly by Shoshanah's parents. She was an only child, so that whoever won her affections won theirs as well; besides which, the boy's own intelligence and good manners made him a favorite. Frau Gertrude Ehrlich, a lady whose health was delicate, took to him especially. She would give him presents that suited the occasion and so did not cause embarrassment; as for the Consul, he helped Jacob's father to meet the cost of his son's schooling, Rechnitz's income not being enough to educate the boy according to his talents. With the Consul's aid Jacob entered high school, and later on, the university.

In his first school year, Jacob spent a good deal of time with Shoshanah. On summer days they made flower chains for one another, which they fitted out with butterflies' wings. In winter they went sliding on the ice-covered pond in the garden. Jacob helped Shoshanah with her lessons, and she taught him to walk on tiptoe and similar accomplishments. In the second year they grew rather more distant.

This was chiefly because Jacob's father had sold his house to satisfy his creditors and rented an apartment in another neighborhood. All that year Jacob was much occupied with his studies, while Shoshanah turned to the more usual pursuits of the daughters of the rich, to music and painting and outdoor sport. Even so, they were not truly separated, for the Consul's wife would invite Jacob to lunch on the first Sunday of every month, as well as on Shoshanah's birthday. This continued until Frau Ehrlich fell sick, and the house was closed to guests, and Shoshanah was sent to a boarding school for girls in another city.

After that, the Consul would invite Jacob twice a year to visit his office. The walls were covered with silk hangings, to which were attached two large portraits, one of his wife and the other of his daughter. Frau Ehrlich wore a long dress whose hem swirled all around the base of the picture. The color of the dress was sky blue, and it fell to the frame fold on fold, so that she seemed to move in a mist. On her head was a small bonnet made up like a kerchief, whose laces lay along the back of her neck. Shoshanah's dress, however, reached only to her knees and her legs seemed to tremble lightly. When the sun lit up the picture she appeared to be on the point of running. Besides these pictures on the wall, two more stood on the table, again of mother and daughter, and before them was set a moist rose in a glass of clear water. The Consul was a man of tidy habits; before receiving visitors he would clear away all papers and ledgers not needed for the occasion, so that it seemed to Jacob, on entering, that the office was built solely in order to house the pictures, with the Consul like an old attendant seated constantly on guard. This impression was confirmed when, after Jacob had sat down, the Consul stood up from his chair and added water to the glass. The boy was always reluctant to raise his eyes above the level of his host's head, as if he had no right to look at the portraits. All the same, they imprinted themselves on his mind, and took on a life of their own: sometimes, he saw Frau Ehrlich vanishing into the mists, and Shoshanah running on and on with a wet rose in her mouth. As for the Consul, he would greet Jacob kindly, remark how he had grown, and address him as if he were another adult.

In winter he would take Jacob to a coffee house where the tableware was of silver and the seats were soft. As soon as the waiter saw the Consul enter, he brought him his coffee, for the Consul was known there and everyone could anticipate his requests. "What shall we order for our young friend?" asked the Consul, beaming at Jacob; he would then call for cocoa with whipped cream and a tray of cakes. They would sit together until dark, and when they parted the Consul would bid him convey greetings to his father and mother.

In summer he took him riding in a jaunting-car with rubber wheels. They drove out of the city for an hour or so till they reached Katharinenhof, which was fenced round with thick hedges whose fresh green shoots were beginning to darken. They entered a great park with circular flower beds and a statue of the Emperor. Somewhere about there were cows and cattle sheds, but you could neither see them nor smell them; behind the park was a view of mountain peaks, with the odor of pine trees drifting down, and the whole park seemed on holiday. They would sit down with the new-mown grass like mats at their feet and drink the excellent coffee for which this place was famous. The cream stood on it like a dollop of snow just ready to melt; and with the coffee there were little cakes to eat, made with cheese and poppy seeds and raisins; or else there was rye bread whose very smell made you hungry, and whose taste made you strong. They served it with fresh, creamy butter glistening with drops of water. Afterwards, the Consul lit a cigar and talked to Jacob about his studies; then, when the cigar was smoked, he lit a fresh one, rose from the table and said "Let's go," in a tone implying that enough time had been spent on pleasure, and now business called. Jacob got up hurriedly, watched the proprietor help the Consul on with his coat and blushed with embarrassment as the man came over to assist him too. He looked down at the ground, asking after the health of Frau Ehrlich. The Consul removed the cigar from his lips and was silent for a moment; then he said, "I wish I could tell you that she is well." Since he could not quite say that, yet did not wish to leave Jacob sad, he added, "Shoshanah, though, as I see from her letters, does very well." And Jacob, duly inclining his head, replied, "Please convey my best wishes to the gentle Fräulein." – "I shall do that," Shoshanah's father replied, in a tone suggesting that this was a task not lightly performed, but one which he would see carried out.

IV

In time Jacob left high school for the university. His father's financial affairs had improved, and he himself could now earn his keep by tutoring. He no longer needed the Consul's aid, but his affection for the older man still kept the twice-yearly meeting a fixture. When they parted the Consul would take out his pocket book, note down the next date and time, and remark, 'So, in another six months! However, you must telephone my office beforehand." Lest that should sound like a veiled intention to put Jacob off, he would pause, add the months up, and conclude, "Well, in another half-year!"

Once, when Rechnitz telephoned on the prearranged day, he was told that the Consul was engaged and would not be available. Instead, he was asked to call a day or two later. Next day, when he was teaching one of his pupils, the boy's father asked Jacob to repeat the name of the consul he had once mentioned in conversation, and then showed Jacob a newspaper, pointing to an obituary notice. "Tomorrow," he added, "you will be going to the funeral of the Consul's wife."

All that night Jacob Rechnitz lay awake. Days that had gone now stood before him, days in and out of the Consul's house, when the Consul's wife had shown him so much kindness, in her ways and in her words. Jacob's mother, too, had loved him as a mother should love her son, and he had returned her love in a son's normal way; but his affection for Frau Gertrude Ehrlich was something apart. It was a love that could be accounted for by no natural cause, though there was reason for it, no doubt, as there is reason for all things; yet the reason was forgotten, the cause was lost and only the effect remained. He had known, indeed, that Frau Ehrlich was an invalid, and this had troubled and saddened him; but never had he been so grieved as on that night, in his awareness of her death. Shoshanah was now orphaned of her mother. That Shoshanah's mother was dead, that she herself was an orphan, did not evoke in him any feeling of pity; it was rather like a new motion of the soul, when the soul attaches itself at once to one who is absent and another who is present, and is taken up into both as one.

Before daybreak Jacob Rechnitz had risen and made his way to the cemetery. In the press of his nighttime thoughts Jacob was sure that he had missed the funeral, though if he hurried he might yet arrive in time to see the last of the actual burial. The cemetery gates were open and he could hear the sound of digging among the graves. He ran forward between the trees and the tombstones in the direction of the sound. Two men were at work, standing up to their waists in the earth; a third was pacing out the length of the grave. When the diggers noticed Rechnitz, they looked up. "Do you want to see if it fits you?" they asked, indicating with their spades that he was free to step into the grave. Rechnitz did not understand them and did not move. The man pacing out the grave asked him what he had come for. Rechnitz looked at him in amazement: how could he ask such a question! When at last he realized that Frau Ehrlich's body still lay in the house, it was almost as if he had heard good news. Though she was dead, she was at least above ground.

Before the entrance to the Ehrlichs' villa men and women stood in silence. There are times and places when the tongue is tied even in company. Jacob's mother stroked his cheek and wiped away a tear; his father pressed his foot into the ground as though testing for a foundation. Suddenly the gates opened and men in black mourning clothes brought out the bier, laying it in a black hearse to which four black horses were harnessed. The scent of flowers floated across from the wreaths on and about the bier. The sound of muffled weeping mingled with the scent; an old servant had covered her mouth with a handkerchief so as not to be heard. While the hearse was being made ready for the journey, Shoshanah and her father came out. Shoshanah wore black, with a black veil over her face, her arm in her father's arm. Both walked as if set apart from this world. Involuntarily, Jacob took a step forward that she might see him, but then as quickly stepped back. Along that funeral way Shoshanah did not once raise her eyes from her mother's bier. And since the bereaved had requested in newspaper notices that there should be no condolence visits, Jacob sent a letter of condolence instead.

V

As we have said, Jacob Rechnitz set out for the Land of Israel, financed in part by the prize he had won from the university, in part by the Consul's aid; for when his course was completed and his doctorate granted, Ehrlich invited him to dine out in celebration, and presented him with a sum of money which saved him from the immediate necessity of seeking a post. The gift was made to seem not a matter of financial aid but rather a token of affection and esteem. It was in keeping with all that the Consul had done for him, and touched him so deeply that a refusal was out of the question. Rechnitz put the two sums together, and joined a party traveling to the Land of Israel; there he found work as a schoolteacher, and settled in Jaffa.

He did not forget his benefactor. Twice a year, at the Jewish and the Christian New Year, Rechnitz sent greetings to the Consul. And when his first article was published, he sent him a reprint. But he never wrote to Shoshanah, for the things that had bound them in childhood no longer counted, now that they were grown.

In brief, Jacob Rechnitz was now teaching at his Jaffa school, shaping the minds of many pupils and playing his part in meetings of teachers and parents. For there were already a few schools which encouraged parents to join in their deliberations, while the teachers in turn were given a chance to have their say in communal affairs. Indeed, when it came to public meetings and discussions, there was not a man in Jaffa who neglected his duty. And yet Rechnitz found time to keep up his special study of marine vegetation, and occasionally to write an article on the subject. There is a time for all, and a season for every desire. All the more so in the days before the Great War, and all the more so in the Land of Israel; for then the days were many times longer than ours, and a man was able to do much more, with hours left over in which to take stock of his world. Ordinary people were tolerably contented, and since they were not obliged to give too much thought to themselves, they had time to spare for other matters.

Rechnitz would frequent the homes of the town intelligentsia, where he was given a warm welcome. If there was a pleasing daughter, that was good; if there were two, better still. There were in fact girls of breath-taking beauty who did not belong to such homes. These, who had come to the country by themselves, without their parents, had set their caps at poets and writers, whereas the daughters of the middle class preferred teachers and scholars, who could make a living by their occupations.

Jacob Rechnitz, as a teacher and scholar, thus came to be acquainted mainly with girls of this type; girls who, like most true daughters of Israel, were graced with good looks and comely bearing and winning ways. Jacob never spoke to them about his work. But he would tell them about other lands and seas, about strange peoples and tribes, their customs and habits, their poetry and myths. So it came to pass that if you heard a girl in Jaffa speaking of Greece and Rome, of Sappho and Medea, you could be sure that she had learned all this from Jacob Rechnitz. Until his arrival, no Jaffa girl had ever heard things of this sort, even though the town was full of men with university degrees who had learned of such matters in their time; for their minds had let it all slip, just as their minds had turned away from what they had studied before that in the yeshivas. But Rechnitz had gained his knowledge in childhood, when the things of the imagination and the works of nature go hand in hand, so that even with the passing of time and the growth of the mind they do not come into conflict. Furthermore, Jacob Rechnitz was a native of Austria, where one is less conscious of the Exile and where one's thoughts are drawn to happier things; and it is the way of these happier thoughts that they give pleasure not only to oneself but to others.

Many girls felt affection for Jacob, just as he felt affection for them. It may well be that some of them had marriage in mind, and Jacob perhaps thought of finding himself a wife, though he could not yet picture himself a married man, or decide who would suit him best. Meanwhile, he would call upon Rachel Heilperin, or take Leah Luria for a stroll, or visit Asnat Magargot, or gossip with Raya Zablodovsky, or chat with Mira Vorbzhitsky, or now and then see Tamara Levi. Sometimes they would all walk out along the beach at night, when the waves kiss the sands and the sky caresses the earth. Because they were seven, that is, Rechnitz and the six girls, and because they walked together at night, the people of the town called them the "Seven Planets."

Their little circle had come into being in the way of all circles. At first, Rechnitz had formed the habit of taking Leah Luria for walks. She had intended to go to Berlin on a visit to her relatives, and was therefore learning German from Jacob. Since conversational practice was all that she needed, they would take their lessons as they strolled by the shore. When her visit to Berlin was canceled, however, they continued their walks; and now Rachel Heilperin began to join them,

for Rachel was Leah's friend, and her father was one of the trustees of
Jacob's school, who would bring Rechnitz over to his home for "an
olive or two." After that, Asnat Magargot attached herself, and then
Raya Zablodovsky and her cousin from St. Petersburg. But when the
cousin began writing verses to her, she broke with him and brought
Mira Vorbzhitsky instead, and Mira brought along Tamara Levi, who
was previously acquainted with Rechnitz because when he first came
to the country, he had lived next door. Thus the "Seven Planets" were
constituted; and as seven planets they admitted no others, lest they
lose claim to the title.

VI

One day before Hanukah a letter from Africa came for Jacob Rechnitz. It was from Herr Gotthold Ehrlich. For a year now the Consul and his daughter had been on their travels, and since they were
returning by way of Egypt, they wished to visit the Holy Land, and
Jerusalem the Holy City.

Rechnitz was delighted at the news. First, because he would
see the Consul again. Secondly, because this would give him a chance
to make some small return for much kindness. He did not want a
great deal for himself, but one thing he desired was to show gratitude
to his benefactor. Now, with the Consul's coming visit, Jacob could
assume the role of a host and be of service to his guest.

He began to make all sorts of plans. First, he told himself, he
would take a leave from school, so as to be free to show the Consul
his country – Sharon, Galilee, the Jewish people tilling their soil. In
his excitement, he forgot that the Consul had written expressly of his
intention to spend only five or six days in Palestine; in five or six days
one could scarcely take in more than the view a bird has of the sea.

In this time of waiting Rechnitz kept calling up memories
of the Consul and his wife, their home and their hospitality. Again
he saw himself walking with Shoshanah, picking flowers in the garden and plaiting them together, or sliding on the ice of the garden
pond. In his thoughts all the seasons merged, and all the goodness
and grace in them became one. How many summers and winters
had passed since then? Now the villa was locked up, the table was

deserted, and the fruit and flowers of the garden were for no one to see. Frau Ehrlich was dead, and Shoshanah was traveling about the world with her father, who since his bereavement had found no rest, but sought distraction in the very things that leave a man no peace, in constant journeys and wanderings from land to land. Rechnitz remembered the day of the funeral, the black hearse piled high with flowers, swaying slightly as it moved, and Shoshanah following with the black veil over her face. Now, however hard he tried, he could not picture her as a grown woman. But sometimes the veil would lift to reveal her again as a child, running on tiptoe, chasing butterflies in the garden, and threading them into a chain of flowers around her head. How many years had gone, how many years had come, but Jacob still recalled her unforgettable whimsy.

VII

The Consul did not disappoint Rechnitz. He came just when he was expected. One day as Jacob entered the school staff-room he saw awaiting him there a well-dressed, elderly man, accompanied by a tall and attractive girl. After Jacob had greeted his benefactor, or perhaps even before, Shoshanah offered him her warm, finely-shaped hand and spoke to him as an old friend, using the intimate *du* and looking at him as if she still saw before her the boy he had once been. And yet in her glance there was inquiry as well as remembrance, as of a person seeking to compare present and past. He found himself embarrassed. It had never occurred to him that Shoshanah might address him in terms of easy intimacy. With the beating of his heart and this sense of embarrassment he could not return her gaze. He too thought back to the past, yet without comparing the Shoshanah of those days to the Shoshanah who stood before him now.

Rechnitz had made so many plans for the day of the Consul's arrival; he had seen himself planning everything for the Consul's benefit and pleasure, informing the Consul of arrangements for this day and the next. But now, as he stood facing his benefactor, the plans were all gone from his head, and it was he who waited for directions. The Consul took his watch from his pocket, remarked that it was lunch time and asked Jacob if he were free to join them at their meal. So Jacob followed their lead, sometimes walking to the left of the Consul and sometimes behind Shoshanah, until they reached the hotel.

This was situated in the German Quarter, not far from Rechnitz's school, where it stood in a wide, pleasant garden. There were shrubs and flowers and well grown trees as well as two large citrus groves that extended from the school to the edge of the quarter. Rechnitz had often walked in the garden, alone or with one of his female companions.

Once again, Jacob was a guest at the Consul's table. And although this was not the old home, nor was Frau Gertrude Ehrlich there to preside, he behaved much as he had in the past. He took good care of his manners, and did not rush to speak until he was spoken to. When Herr Ehrlich asked how he was doing he raised his head, and, looking him in the eyes, replied, "I am an instructor in one of the Jewish schools, where I teach a little German and Latin. The salary isn't high, but it's as much as I need since rent is low, food is cheap, and there's no need to spend much on dress: not even the rich do that. This country teaches people to be satisfied with very little and I am satisfied too. What is more, I have found a few intelligent people who, though not scientists themselves, have respect for a man of science." At this point Rechnitz blushed, for he had included himself among "men of science."

"And what of your research work?" asked Ehrlich. Rechnitz replied, "Here there is time for everything; even for useless things, such as my research."

Herr Ehrlich seemed pleased with his answer, which showed at once some knowledge of the world's attitude and a readiness to carry on with his work, and after all somebody ought to have a look into such matters, for Rechnitz's work might have its uses. Shoshanah sat wrapped up in herself. She may or may not have been listening. At least her eyes did not question the value of Rechnitz's work.

Ehrlich poured a glass of wine for Rechnitz and took one himself, saying, "We happened to meet an old scholar on our travels, a professor with a lot of abstruse knowledge. Once I picked up a strange-looking plant from the sea and showed it to him. He said,

'This plant was unknown until a young Austrian research worker stationed in Jaffa discovered it. It's called after him *Caulerpa Rechnitzia*.' Now you are an Austrian, you live in Jaffa, and Rechnitz is your name. Could you be that very man? – *Herr Doktor,* I am very happy that your reputation leads you to be mentioned in out-of-the-way places. Take up your glass, let's drink to your good health and the success of your research!"

Jacob lowered his head and fumbled for the glass, which Shoshanah took up and placed in his hand. Again she sat back in her place. Apart from passing him some dish from time to time, she paid no attention to him. Jacob thought to himself, Evidently she is sorry that she greeted me so warmly at first.

The waiter came up and set before each of them a small cup of black coffee. The aroma mounted. It reminded him of his room, where he would read alone over his drink with nobody's eyes upon him. He looked down at the coffee. A pale, brownish foam bubbled up on its surface. The foam was full of little eyes that flickered like sparks.

"Don't you take sugar?" asked the Consul.

"Oh yes," Jacob answered, but still forgot to take any.

Shoshanah picked up the silver tongs, secured a lump and dropped it into his cup. "Another?" she asked, and caught a second lump.

"Thank you," he said, and began to wonder whether the instinct to recoil from what harms us would not hold Shoshanah back; for if the sugar fell into the full cup, the coffee would spill over. Then again it seemed to him that this was the first lump after all, there was no need to fear, for when the coffee was poured allowance must surely have been made for the sugar.

The Consul took out his cigar case, offered a cigar to Jacob and chose one for himself. Taking Rechnitz's arm he strolled up and down with him, while the smoke rose up until their cigars were half burnt out, though ash still stood on the tips. The Consul halted in the middle of the lounge, removed his ash, and said, "So here we are, seated together again." Suiting action to word, he walked across to the sofa and sat down opposite Shoshanah, settling Jacob beside him on his right.

He looked across at his daughter, then turned to Jacob, saying, "I'm sure you are busy in the afternoon, so come around this evening and we'll dine together. Wouldn't that be nice, Shoshanah?"

Shoshanah inclined her head in agreement. Evidently her mind was not on what she was doing, but all the same the gesture, however unaware, was pleasant to see.

Actually Rechnitz was free that afternoon, but since the Consul had declared him to be busy he could hardly contradict him. He recalled something he had read in some book of philosophy: how those motions of the soul that urge us on cannot bring us to act without the help of other, external factors. And if these external factors do not collaborate, all the motions of our soul are vain, and lead only to inner confusion. Rechnitz could indeed have consoled himself in the knowledge that he would be returning for supper; but he found no comfort in this, for the barren hours seemed to stretch on endlessly till evening.

Stripped of all cheer, he walked away from the hotel. He said to himself: Since they are here, I will do everything I can. But if they go, let them go. I will have a clear mind again. Why give myself needless cares? What is needless is not needed. I shall try to do what is right, and that is enough. Don't blame me, Shoshanah, if you were mistaken in me, if you thought I still deserved the love you had for me once. We aren't children at play anymore, but grown persons who have known the years. What a pity we aren't happy now!

VIII

A free afternoon. On free days, or at least on free afternoons, Rechnitz would stay in his room, make coffee for himself and read a book. When he had had enough of reading, he would get up to sort out his specimens, or take a walk by the shore in search of new ones. But today he felt no inclination to go home. He had already had coffee, and that deprived him of half his satisfaction, which lay in the pleasure of preparation. He would put the pot on to heat, watch the flames rise through the perforations in the burner and envelop the pot, while the water bubbled and boiled, rose and fell, and he would shake the coffee grounds down on the water and smell the aroma that filled his room. The only alternative was to walk by the sea. Yet a walk by the sea did not appeal to him much. He had overeaten at the hotel; perhaps, too, he felt weighted down by the wine he had drunk. Some of the things he had said in the Consul's presence came back to his mind, and although he didn't exactly find fault with them, an unaccountable sadness took hold of him. His fancy wandered and returned, but he lacked the power to center his thoughts on one subject.

Leah Luria came by and saw Rechnitz alone. "Sir, you stand in the markets of Jaffa as if the world were yours," she said.

Rechnitz buttoned up his coat and replied, "I feel more as if there were no place for me in the world."

Leah stared at him with her two fine eyes. "I hope to God that nothing has gone wrong, Doctor." Her voice was full of distress and concern, and a will to hit upon some good advice or suggestion. Her face, too, spoke of a longing to advise him, to save him from trouble.

Rechnitz shook his head. "Nothing's wrong at all, but when a man finds himself idle in the middle of the day, then he surely doesn't know what to do."

Leah said, "If a walk is something to do, we can walk for a while; only I promised to call on Rachel Heilperin. Let's go over to her place, perhaps she will come too." She looked at the watch on her wrist. "She must be waiting for me now. Would you come with me?"

Rechnitz answered with a little singsong, "And why not?"

She laughed. "Let's go, then."

"Come on." It hardly mattered whether he walked with one or with both of them, so long as it made his heart a little lighter.

Even though Leah Luria had given up studying German conversation when she gave up her trip to Berlin the year before, she and Jacob still kept to their walks. Anyone who saw them together would say that there went a perfect couple. And perhaps Jacob and Leah thought the same, each in his own way; except that Jacob thought similarly, or not very differently, about himself and Rachel Heilperin, and perhaps about himself and another, as we shall soon see. And perhaps these others, too, were of the same opinion, each in her own fashion.

Leah was not very young; she was already twenty-three or four. Her features were full, her face was neither too long nor too round, her forehead was smooth. She had ash-blonde hair and a full body, which she carried with such dignity as to impress everyone she met. She herself could never understand the attentions she received, and her manner suggested surprise; while, out of fear that she might bore her companions, she spoke little. Yet this very reticence added to her charm; for she gave the impression that if only she were to speak, one would hear words of wisdom. Her complexion was on the dark side; she wore a bright turquoise dress with a light chain round her neck, and thick-soled country shoes which added to her height and loosened her stride. Her arms were round and warm, her eyes seemed pleased at all you did. And even though these eyes might at first appear to be astonished, it was clear in the end that they approved of whatever you did. Why, you may ask, had Leah not found her partner in life? Because Rachel was the more beautiful girl. Tall and slender as a palm tree, to use the biblical image, without an ounce of fat on her flesh. Her eyes would light up occasionally, though for the most part they expressed chill indifference, and her lips would smile in such a way that you would gladly give her your heart, even before she took it for herself. Why then had Rachel not found her partner? Perhaps because of Leah, who demanded nothing of you, and in demanding nothing, led you to want to give her all. The reason for this is not as clear as it might be, but despite the confusion, it works strangely on the soul.

IX

Rachel and Leah were girls of good family, whose fathers had their place in the history of the Zionist Return. One of them was a correspondent of the great Ahad Ha'Am, who addressed him as "My esteemed friend." The other's opinions carried weight with the Odessa Council, and even with Lilienblum and Ussishkin.

Much had happened in the lives of both men. Yehiel Luria, the father of Leah, had begun as a yeshiva student, devoting himself to the Torah in the traditional fashion; at times for its own sake, at times for the security afforded by a rabbi's life, at times for the prestige it carried, and at times because he could imagine no possible way of life without the Torah. But winds of change began to blow through the yeshiva walls; among them, a purifying wind that brought new promise of national revival. The students of the yeshiva began to speak of God's prophecies, of the return to Zion and the sprouting of the horn of salvation for the house of Israel in the Holy Land. Some of them were later to betray their own words; others had the privilege of fulfilling in their lives what they sought after in their hearts. And when Yehiel heard that in the Land of Israel there were Jews who lived upon the soil, he resolved to go there and fulfill the Torah through working the land. He saw himself joining a settlement and becoming a farmer, sowing seed with one hand and holding his Talmud in the other; or following the plough with his copy of the Jerusalem Talmud resting upon it, thus at once fulfilling the Torah of the Land of Israel and the working of its soil. When his time came to be drafted into the Tsar's army, he fled for the Land of Israel and entered one of the yeshivas in Jerusalem. He had thus achieved the merit of following the Torah; but not of fulfilling it through toil, for the yeshivas were remote from the pioneer community in spirit, and work on the land was considered profane by the people of Jerusalem. He went on with his studies, much as he had done outside the country, except that there he had had great hopes for his life in the Land of Israel, whereas in the Holy Land itself half his hopes were gone. And now he was a married man and father of a daughter; he began to think hard of the practical future. He took what remained of his wife's dowry and went into business. The result was that he lost her money and was left with nothing but the Torah he had learned, and even that was not all it should have been. Once, however, he happened to accompany a collector of donations and tithes who was making his rounds of the settlements. He saw the Jewish people at work in the fields and vineyards, and although in those days the settlers were held in ill repute among the people of Jerusalem, Yehiel ignored all this and hired himself out to one of the farmers. He turned himself into a working man, and suffered what had to be suffered, and rejoiced that at last he had been privileged to till the holy soil. But not long afterwards, the farmers of the settlements assigned their land to Baron Rothschild's officials, and all the joy was gone from their work. Yehiel

went away to another place, and then to yet another, until his wanderings brought him to upper Galilee, where he became a teacher.
He spent himself in that effort, but received no satisfaction from it,
for his pupils did not respond to what he tried to teach. So he left
his school and went down to Jaffa, and with the help of his wife's
relatives in Berlin started a shop for spades, pruning hooks and other
tools needed on the land. Anyone coming from the villages found in
him a friend and comrade and a good counselor.

Very different was the story of Boris Heilperin, Rachel's father.
From early childhood he had received a modern education, and when
he finished his studies, he became manager of a brickyard. His home
was a meeting place for the Lovers of Zion, and later, for the "Political Zionists."

In the great Uganda schism, Heilperin suddenly resigned from
his post in the brick works and left behind him both groups, the
"Zionists" and the "Zionists of Zion." With his family he emigrated to
the Land of Israel and joined a pioneer settlement that had a number
of members of the Bilu group, with whom he had exchanged cordial
letters. But not long passed before a dispute flared up among them.
Heilperin said to himself, If I cannot live in harmony among these
comrades, to whom I am bound in heart and soul, how much less
so will I be able to live with the rest of my countrymen? So he went
and rented fields from an Arab, and he and his household worked
the land as ordinary farmers, until his children were grown to school
age. Now there was no school within the village or anywhere near it;
so he left his farm land and came to Jaffa, and opened a shop there
for lime, cement and construction materials. There was no blessing
on his business for the same reason that Luria had none: neither was
accustomed to commerce, and it was a time of recession. Also, they
gave their attention to the affairs of the Jewish Settlement rather
than to their own. All the same they were content with their lot,
and offered thanks, one to God, the other to Fate, that they were
privileged to live in the Land of Israel. Though their views differed,
they respected one another. Luria held Heilperin in esteem for his
determination, and Heilperin esteemed Luria for his integrity, while
the newer generation respected them both, not only for these virtues

but just because they were "respected." Their homes were open to all, teachers and writers were warmly welcomed. From four o'clock until ten at night the samovar was lit and tea awaited you. Both men had a liking for Dr. Rechnitz. Rachel's father forgave him for coming from the Austro-Hungarian Empire and for not speaking Russian. Leah's father was even glad of this; he would not have minded, in fact, had Rechnitz come from Galicia, since he had married a Galician woman himself. Like the enlightened people they were, they did not try to rush Rechnitz into declaring his intentions, but waited patiently for that moment on which the fathers of daughters set all their hopes.

x

Rachel had already heard from her brother, who was a pupil at the school where Rechnitz taught, that important visitors had called on his teacher. An old gentleman and a grown girl. The old gentleman stooped, like all men of his age from abroad. But the girl was tall and lovely. The clothes she wore were not to be seen anywhere in the Land of Israel.

Rachel said to Rechnitz, "I hear you have guests." He nodded.

"Who are they?" she asked.

"People from my city."

"And who is the girl?"

"She's the daughter of the old gentleman."

"Is she beautiful?"

"That depends on one's taste."

"My brother has told me about her."

Rechnitz looked up. "What did he say?"

"Why don't you tell us a little yourself? You're very silent."

"There's not much to tell. When I was a boy, our house was next to that of Herr Ehrlich, and I used to be in and out of his home, as happens with neighbors. When Frau Ehrlich died, and even before then, when my parents moved elsewhere, I gave up visiting, because of the distance and because we weren't on the same neighborly terms. Now it happens that the Consul and his daughter are traveling around the world, and on their way back from Africa they are spending four or five days in the Land of Israel."

"And what about her?" asked Rachel. "I mean, the Consul's daughter?"

"She's with her father; and on their way home they have come to see the Holy Land."

Rachel smiled rather mysteriously; her eyes resumed their usual look of indifference. Rechnitz blushed. He thought of the many favors the Consul had done him; yet he had shown little gratitude by this offhand way of referring to him. He looked across at Leah.

"Leave him alone, Rachel," said Leah. "Can't you see that Dr. Rechnitz has nothing to say?"

"He may have nothing on his tongue," said Rachel, "but I think he has something on his mind. Tell us about it, Doctor."

"She is the daughter of my benefactor."

His tone of voice startled Rachel. She began to make some remark, reconsidered, and said instead, "If I may ask, how long have you been acquainted with her? You were neighbors, weren't you?"

Rechnitz answered, "We were neighbors when we were children, but I haven't seen her since I started high school."

"Interesting, *most* interesting," said Rachel.

"What's so interesting?" asked Leah.

"It is, don't you agree, Doctor?"

Leah said, "We'd do better to go for our walk. It's a shame to waste time indoors. Are you ready, Rachel?"

"Yes, ready."—"And so?"—"So, let's go."— "Where to?"—"Oh, wherever our feet take us. Doctor, what do you say? Shall we go to Mikveh? Or to Sarona?"

Rechnitz said, "I'm invited to dinner, so I can't go very far."

Rachel laughed. "It's not an hour since he left her, and he already wants to be back."

Rechnitz looked at the clock. "Anyway," he said, "I have time for a short walk."

"I'll take it upon myself," said Leah, "to bring you back to the place you have to be at the time you have to be there."

They turned and took their way along the sea, as people in Jaffa do when they have no special destination.

XI

The sand, neither too loose nor too hard-packed, gave off a good smell. And above the sand, though not too far from earth, the sky was full of fresh clouds, half of them lead tinged with silver, and half, red gold. Over these were smaller clouds; some the shape of beasts or birds, and some rising like the rays of sunrise. Mists of sulphur veiled them, mists that were torn, then opened, that wheeled and then moved on. The noise of the waves mounted, the sea was full, casting up numberless new conches and shells on the margin of the beach, like some being that lacked peace in its depths.

Rachel picked up a hollow shell and held it to her ear. Leah was about to make some remark but thought better of it and said nothing. She stooped to lift up a shell, whispered into it and threw it into the sea. Rechnitz picked up a plant that the waves had left, inspected it, and remarked, "I forgot to ask what time dinner is served."

Rachel looked at him as if she didn't know where things were heading. "Are you so hungry?"

"No, but…"

She laughed. "Well, let's ask."

He nodded. "Yes, of course; we had better go."

Leah gazed at the sea. "How lovely it is. It's a pity we have to leave."

"I can promise you," smiled Rachel, "that the sea won't run away between now and tomorrow."

"I suppose so," Leah answered, still looking out to sea.

"Don't you believe me?"

Leah laughed. "All right, let's go."

They walked back and reached the hotel. Shoshanah was taking a walk on the grounds. Rachel halted suddenly and stared straight in front of her. Finally she pressed a hand to her brow and exclaimed, "How lovely that girl is! Who is she?"

Rechnitz silenced her and whispered, "That's she; that's the Consul's daughter."

"Oh indeed," answered Rachel in a different tone. "It's clear that she's haughty!"

"How do you know that?" said Leah.

"How do I know that she's haughty? Didn't you see that motion of her head when she returned Dr. Rechnitz's greeting?"

Jacob, however, recognized the gesture; she had inclined her head similarly when the Consul invited him to dinner. Such movements are unwilled: they do not come from our awareness, nor from the soul, which normally govern our gestures.

Leah glanced down at Jacob's hands. "You are going to your meeting empty-handed. Where can we get you some flowers to bring to your guests?"

Jacob was dismayed. He should indeed have thought of this, but he had made no preparations for his visitors. He looked hopefully at Leah, who gazed at the flower beds in front of the hotel entrance and commiserated with him.

Rachel suggested, "Mira lives only a few steps away; and if she's not at home, we can try Raya. Her Petersburg cousin just smothers her in flowers. Don't worry, Dr. Rechnitz; we shan't send you along empty-handed."

Rechnitz glanced at her imploringly, took off his hat in gratitude, and cried, "Thank you!"

Rachel continued, "If it weren't for that fine lady in the garden, I might have fetched some flowers from the porter. There's nothing lovelier than white narcissus in the hands of a black African. Why are you silent, Dr. Rechnitz? Tell us a story, like that one about the African queen who used to come to her council of state riding on the back of one of her ministers."

Leah hugged her, exclaiming, "You are a good little girl, Rachel!"

"Aren't I? Taking the flowers that Raya's cousin brings her and sending them to that fine lady by means of Dr. Rechnitz! It would be still better if they were Mira's flowers originally, which *she* had given first to the cousin! Forgive me, Dr. Rechnitz, I really don't mean any harm. Shake hands and let's make up. Aren't you feeling cold, Leah?" Rachel slipped an arm around her friend's shoulder and kissed her on the neck. "Your neck tastes salty, Leah."

In return Leah embraced Rachel, kissed her warmly and said, "I don't know what's the matter with me. I can't say that I am happy, but I can say that things seem good."

"If they seem good they *are* good," said Rachel. "For my part, I really don't know what's good and what isn't."

With her eyes on the ground, Leah pondered what her friend had said.

XII

Rechnitz arrived about half an hour before the meal. Shoshanah was standing near the entrance, examining the picture postcards which the hotel clerk had set out before her. Seeing Jacob, she greeted him with a nod and returned to her postcards, laying some down for a second inspection. The Consul was below in the reading room, looking over a newspaper. He caught sight of Rechnitz, removed the cigar from his lips, put his paper down on the table, and extended his hand.

"I'm sorry to interrupt your reading," Rechnitz remarked.

The Consul took off his spectacles. "There's no news. The world carries on as usual, the newspapers likewise. They make us participate in the world's affairs according to their own notions. These newspapers unite mankind; they make opinions uniform. True, they may disagree among themselves, but their very disagreements prove that their outlook is basically the same and that they only differ on details. In the future, all human beings will be alike, except perhaps the savages in Africa – *they* may keep some of the individuality that God planted in the hearts of His creatures. Well, well! I'm philosophizing. All the same, there's a grain of truth in what I say, even if it sounds like armchair philosophy. But you, I am sure, have found interesting people here!"

At this point the Consul called over a waiter and told him to reserve a special table for them at dinner, adding that if this were not feasible, they would wait until all the guests had finished their meal. Turning back to Rechnitz, he said, "That is to say, if you are not hungry. What were we talking about before? The press, was it? No, it was about people. Have you found interesting people here?"

"Where are people not interesting? It seems to me that every man has his appeal. Perhaps this is because I am not well acquainted with human nature and don't know many people. And perhaps it is because most of the people in Jaffa are Russian Jews. And most of the Russians are lively – in mind and in body: they never get involved in one all-absorbing interest, with the exception of arguments; in that respect, of course, they are all alike."

The Consul flicked his cigar ash into the tray before him. "If you live another year among these Russians, you'll see that they, too, are like everyone else. What do they argue about? What is there that's worth arguing about?"

"It's enough for one of them to make a remark, and the other starts an argument at once. And even if they're both on the same side, there won't be a thing said without a grand debate."

"Most interesting," said the Consul.

Rechnitz watched him concentrate on trying to drop the unconsumed ash, and went on, "The facts in themselves may not be of special interest, but the process is interesting, since it repeats itself no matter what the circumstances may be, and one knows from the start that whatever Mr. Greenberg says will be contradicted by Mr. Berggreen."

Ehrlich smiled. "You made up those names, my dear fellow."

"Well," said Rechnitz, "it's true that nobody here is called Greenberg or Berggreen, but a number of people have names that are the reverse of one another."

"And what about the Sefardim?" the Consul asked.

"I'm not acquainted with them. They stay in their own homes and don't mix with the Ashkenazim. Perhaps they lack a social sense. Besides, they regard themselves as kings who have been deposed and are angry at us Ashkenazim for presuming to reign in their place. But I know the Yemenite Jews a little. They're a nimble, quick-witted tribe, who love work and are very studious and pious too. We have a Yemenite caretaker at our school. He has the face of a prince, and everything he sees sets his mind working. Once he asked me, 'Why is it that King David says: *Thou hast set a boundary, they shall not cross it, they shall not return to cover the earth?* God has set a boundary to the waters of the sea, that they shall not go up on the dry land. And yet we see that the waters of the sea do go up on the dry land.'"

"And how did you answer the Yemenite?"

"What could I reply?" said Rechnitz. "I didn't give him any answer, but I sighed deeply, as one does when regretting that things are not as they should be."

"That's the best answer of all," the Consul said. "But here I'm smoking, and I haven't offered you a cigar. Actually it's a sin to smoke tobacco in this wonderful fragrant air. But what can I do? It's my addiction. If I'm reading a newspaper or talking to someone, of course I smoke. And if I'm neither reading nor talking, I smoke out of sheer boredom." He laughed in the way people do who make fun of their own weaknesses and yet are quite contented with them. "Well, if you don't want a cigar, let's have a sip of brandy."

The Consul tasted some brandy. "Not bad, really," he commented. After a second glass he gave it fuller praise.

"This brandy," said Rechnitz, "comes from Rishon LeZion. How about our going there, sir? You will see a great wine press that has no equal in Europe."

The Consul smiled a little patronizingly. "I doubt if I shall have time. After all, one can't visit the Holy Land and not go to Jerusalem, and we've only another four days. You must have been there already. Some tourists I met on the way were not impressed with Jerusalem, you know. Dirt and beggars, they said; nothing but beggars and dirt."

"Were they Christian or Jewish tourists?"

"What does that matter? It's a holy land for Christians, too."

The conversation then took a strange turn. Rechnitz blushed and said nothing.

"If the air of Jerusalem is as fine as that of Jaffa," said the Consul, "that will be good enough. I've not found the like of it anywhere. And the old Baron says so too. Do you know him? He was a general in Africa, or a governor for his king, or some such dignitary. What do you think, Jacob? Shall I settle down here? My late father's grandfather came to Jerusalem an old man, and passed away there at the end of a ripe old age. I remember when I was a child, a charity collector from Jerusalem came to the house and my father gave him money. And every year printed matter used to come from there, and every Rosh Hashanah eve my father would send a contribution. I was approached, too, on behalf of the Land of Israel; they tried to get me to buy shares in the Settlement Bank. I said to them, 'If it's charity you want, I'm ready to give you something; but what have "settlement shares" to do with the Holy Land? Old men go there to die, but what have young men to go for?' – I'm not referring to you, my friend; you came for the sake of your research, and science has its place everywhere!"

As Rechnitz was about to reply, the waiter came up to announce that their table was ready. The Consul nodded, and said, "We have been talking for a good while now, and all the guests should have had time to finish their meal. Waiter, see if my daughter is ready for dinner."

XIII

When the three of them were seated at dinner, the Consul turned to Shoshanah and asked, "Well daughter, how did you spend your day? I don't think I've seen you since we finished lunch."

Shoshanah replied, "Ask our guest that question: he will tell you."

"How should Dr. Rechnitz know?"

Jacob lowered his head as his host asked, "Well Doctor, how did our friend Fräulein Shoshanah Ehrlich spend her day?"

What did Rechnitz know about Shoshanah's doings? For a brief moment he had caught a glimpse of her in the garden while he was walking with Rachel and Leah, before she disappeared, leaving him nothing to remember but her nod. He looked at her in perplexity.

The Consul smiled. "Evidently you have a secret between you. Well now, let's ask Dr. Rechnitz how *his* day was spent."

Now, thought Rechnitz to himself, I suppose Shoshanah will say, "Ask me." But Shoshanah said nothing.

The Consul filled their glasses and drank to their health. As Rechnitz drank, he reflected on how tomorrow they would be traveling on to Jerusalem and he would return to his own affairs. And how they would come back to Jaffa, and leave again.

Shoshanah was seated on the Consul's left, facing Jacob. Her spirit seemed to have sunk deep down into her being, or to have fled her body entirely. A light breeze was blowing in; the scent of lemon and orange trees filled the dining room. The lamp on the table shone with double brightness, and the sides of its white base grew red. From the gardens and the citrus groves came the cry of jackals, and the parrot in its cage stirred itself to echo their high-pitched screams. Suddenly the sea awoke; its waves pounded and a pleasant sea smell mingled with the fragrance from the gardens and groves that girdle Jaffa.

The Consul raised his glass: "Go tell my countrymen that while they're sitting over their cabbage with their blood congealing from the cold, we here take dinner by the open window! Are you cold, Shoshanah? What are you bringing us now, waiter – black coffee? If I drink coffee at night, I can't sleep. Every age has its own customs: our forefathers used to take drinks that put them to sleep, but now we try to keep ourselves awake. After all, is there anything in the world worth staying awake for? Those scents from the garden are most exhilarating: a mixture of jasmine and orange blossom, isn't it?"

Shoshanah sat in silence. Those exhilarating scents were putting her to sleep. Without a word, she stood up from the table and kissed her father's brow.

"Are you going up to your room, my daughter?" he asked.

"Yes, Papa."

Herr Ehrlich kissed her on the cheek and said good night. Shoshanah gave her hand to Jacob, then left.

The Consul watched her leave and said, "Shoshanah is rather tired; I don't think we shall go to Jerusalem tomorrow. What will you be doing?"

Rechnitz consulted his diary. "I am free tomorrow after midday."

"Then come and take lunch with us," said the Consul. "Shoshanah and I are always glad of your company."

"How about our going to Mikveh Israel tomorrow?"

"Where is that?"

"About an hour's walk from here."

"Walk?" echoed the Consul in dismay.

"It's possible to go by carriage. And from there it's an hour's journey to Rishon LeZion."

"And what is Sarona?" asked the Consul.

"Sarona is a small village of Christian Germans."

"Where is it?"

"Very near here."

"I've heard," said the Consul, "that they are very good farmers and God-fearing people. Let's decide tomorrow where we shall go. We'll lunch at half-past twelve. Bring a good appetite with you, it will encourage us to eat, too!"

XIV

When Rechnitz came at noon, Shoshanah was not there. She had spent most of the night looking over the pictures she had bought and had not gone to bed; in the morning she had been seen dozing at her window. Reluctantly she had let her father persuade her to lie down and take a short rest. "Shoshanah won't join us for lunch today," the Consul said.

The meal passed in silence, the Consul eating little and showing no appetite. Evidently, thought Rechnitz, he is feeling out of sorts. All the plans to show his visitors around Mikveh Israel and Rishon LeZion came to nothing because of Shoshanah's fatigue.

Over coffee the Consul looked up and said, "Were you about to say something?"

Rechnitz had had no such intention, but since he was called on to speak, he considered for a moment and then said, "Would you like to go, sir, to Mikveh Israel, or to Rishon LeZion?"

"To Mikveh Israel or Rishon LeZion?" the Consul repeated. "After all the places we have been to, a little village like Rishon LeZion, or an agricultural school like Mikveh Israel, doesn't amount to much. Tell me, incidentally, why on earth do you give your settlements such long, double-barreled names? Our forefathers, who lived to a good old age, chose short, agreeable place-names, like Jaffa, Haifa, Acre, Gaza; and you people, who know that your time is brief, do just the opposite."

When Jacob was about to go, Shoshanah appeared. Her face was flushed, her movements sluggish. For seven whole hours, from eight in the morning until now, she had slept without a break, until the maid had brought lunch to her in bed.

"Are you leaving?" she said to Jacob.

"Yes," he replied in a whisper, as if afraid he would wake her.

Shoshanah said, "Come back in an hour, perhaps we'll take a walk."

Jacob looked at the clock, took note of the time, and promised to come.

Within an hour he was back. Shoshanah was seated downstairs in the hotel, dressed in warm clothes, gazing at a lithograph on the wall. When Jacob arrived she looked at him with the same gaze, as if he were part of the picture, or the wall itself on which the picture hung.

He bowed to her. "You wished to go for a walk, did you not?"

"For a walk?" she repeated, as if surprised.

"But surely you said you would like to take a walk?"

Shoshanah stared at him as if he were trying to trick her, then stood up and said, "Very well, let's go."

XV

Shoshanah walked in silence, and Jacob at her side was silent too. Words would not come for all the things he wanted to tell her. It seemed impossible, though, to go on walking in this fashion, and he searched for a subject to draw her attention. At that moment an Arab crossed their path. A member of some ascetic sect, he was barefooted and naked from the waist up. Two lances were embedded in his loins; his hair was long and unkempt; his eyes blazed with zeal. As he walked, he twisted the lances in his flesh, crying out *Allah kareem*; while a great company followed him, repeating, *Allah kareem!* Rechnitz halted and translated the words for Shoshanah. She did not look at the ascetic and paid no attention to his cry. Soon they came to the "Nine Palm Trees," planted by Japheth, the son of Noah, when he founded Jaffa: one for himself, one for his wife, and seven for his seven sons. When

Nebuchadnezzar laid the country waste he uprooted these trees and planted them in his own garden; but when the Jews returned from their Babylonian exile they brought them back and replanted them on the original site. This grove of nine palms, whose fresh green arch seemed to support the silvery clouds, made a crown of green and silver fronds that rustled and glistened, their colors alternating as the light breeze stirred them in their airy cavern, while the fibers of the fronds quivered like raindrops in a sunshower. The sight never failed to move Rechnitz, and especially now when he had the opportunity of pointing it out to Shoshanah. He stretched out his arm, crying, "Look, Shoshanah!" Shoshanah nodded, without a glance either at him or at the palms.

Why am I showing her all this? he asked himself, distressed that he had taken her walking when she was so tired. Aloud he said, "Perhaps you would like to go back to the hotel?"

She nodded her head in agreement. "Yes. But first let's walk by the sea. It's quite near, isn't it?"

She raised her long skirt a little as they made their way.

The sea was still and very blue; the waves broke over one another, raising their crests as if held back from mingling with the waters beneath. Yesterday, the tide was full; now the sea withdrew from the shore, leaving a wide beach. No one was there, except for a single fisherman. Jacob would have given the world in return for something that might draw Shoshanah's attention. But nothing in the world could awaken this sleeping princess who walked by his side, insensible to his presence. Jacob called to mind the times when he had played with Shoshanah in her father's garden, and they had fed the goldfish in the pool. But as he watched the sea and the lonely fisherman standing up to his waist in water, he could not bring himself to speak of things past.

Shoshanah halted suddenly. "Do you remember how you and I used to play in our garden?"

He answered in a whisper, "I remember."

"Good," said Shoshanah. "Let's go on."

Then again she stopped. "Do you remember what games we played?"

Jacob began to recount them to her as he walked. She nodded her head at every detail, saying, "That's right, that's right. I thought you had forgotten."

He laid his hand over his heart, as if to say, "How could anyone forget such things?"

Shoshanah fell silent, but continued to walk, and Jacob followed at her side.

"Aren't you tired?" he asked.

Shoshanah replied, "No, no. What's over there?"

"An old Moslem cemetery."

"Do they still bury their dead there?"

"I have heard that they don't anymore."

"Let's go there," said Shoshanah.

When they reached the cemetery, Shoshanah stopped. "Do you remember that vow we made together?"

"I remember," said Jacob.

She looked at him steadily for a moment. "Do you remember the words of the vow?"

"I remember them," said Jacob.

"Word for word?"

"Yes, word for word."

"If you remember the vow, repeat it."

Jacob repeated the substance of what they had sworn.

"But you told me," said Shoshanah, "that you remember it word for word. Say it to me, then, word for word."

He hesitated, sighed, and at last said: "We swear by fire and by water, by the hair of our heads, by the blood of our hearts, that we shall marry one another and be husband and wife, and no power on earth can cancel our vow, forever and ever."

Shoshanah nodded her head in silence. After a while she said, "Now we can go."

They walked on; then she stopped again. "And what do you think, Jacob? Are we now exempt from that vow?"

His heart pounded so that he was unable to speak.

"Jacob," she said to him, "do you stand by your word?"

Still he stared at her without speaking.

"Are you prepared to keep your vow?" said Shoshanah.

Jacob cried out loudly, "Yes, I am, I am!"

"Good," said Shoshanah. "Let us go back to the hotel."

On the way she stretched out her hand to him, saying goodbye.

"Don't you want me to see you back?" said Jacob.

"It's not necessary."

"You may lose your way."

"I shall never lose my way," said Shoshanah. "I never forget any place I have been; not even in my sleep."

A slight shudder ran through Rechnitz; the roots of his hair tingled. He whispered, "But still…"

"If you really want to come, then do so. But don't speak on the way. I want to do some thinking."

When they came to the hotel, she offered her hand to her betrothed and said goodbye.

XVI

Rechnitz shook himself out of a deep sleep. If you are told that people have a way of turning in their beds, you must not believe that this applied to Rechnitz, at least not that particular night. From the time he went to bed until the time he got up, he lay still as a post.

This fine sleep was the result of his afternoon walk with Shoshanah along the beach. Now he put out his hand, picked up his watch and looked at it as if he were gazing through a soft curtain. "God above," he cried, "if my watch isn't playing tricks, I'll have to run all the way to school just as I am!"

But to run to school without dressing is impossible, and a man also has to wash himself. Accordingly, when Rechnitz had jumped out of bed he filled a basin with cold water, plunged his head into it, and after washing, shaved himself too. Asclepius the god of health protected him, so that he escaped from slashes on the chin or cuts on the cheek. Finally, he put his wet shaving kit down on the bed, threw on his clothes and raced off toward the school.

The pupils were all gathered in the yard and the corridor. Some were munching at the snacks they had brought, some were improvising comic rhymes to set each other laughing. With all the noise, they overlooked the caretaker who was standing in the doorway ready to ring the bell. When they caught sight of him at last, they crowded around, taking hold of his arm, some to hinder and some to help in the ringing. In the meantime Rechnitz arrived and they followed him into the classroom.

Soon they were seated in their places. Rechnitz mounted the platform and took all in with a glance. Everyone was present. Rechnitz was in good spirits, as he always was when surrounded by his pupils. He began teaching in that resonant, cheerful voice which the boys and girls of his class liked so much, speaking or reading with a restrained ardor that awakened their enthusiasm, listing on the blackboard any words whose spelling might give them trouble. Had the bell not rung for the second time that day, he would have continued his teaching, and the class would have continued to listen attentively. After the lesson he ran the eraser over the board and went out. Only now did he notice his hunger, remembering that he had not had anything to eat either that morning or on the previous evening.

Rechnitz went into the staff room. The teachers were sitting together, drinking tea or eating the rolls which the caretaker's wife baked for them daily. They dipped the ring-shaped rolls into their tea, sucking away as they read the books set in front of them. Rechnitz drew up his chair alongside them and hummed the tune of the Hapsburg anthem, beating out the rhythm with his knuckles on the table. This fetched Yehia, who greeted him with "What would you like, Rabbi?" The caretaker always called him "Rabbi," because he knew that Rechnitz was a great scholar in secular science; therefore, needless to say, he must also be greatly learned in the Torah; perhaps also because when he first came to Jaffa he had worn a beard.

"What would I like?" repeated Rechnitz. "I should like a full stomach for myself and happiness for you and all Israel."

"God willing," answered the caretaker.

Rechnitz looked up at Yehia's swarthy face and great black eyes. "Make it black coffee in a tall glass."

The caretaker brought it. Rechnitz clasped the sides of the glass in both hands and lowered his head as if he were trying to conceal his expression. He took a sip, added sugar to the coffee, and sipped again, while trying to think of what he had told the Consul about Yehia. Then he drained his glass. The teachers got up and went off to their classrooms, and he too made his way out.

Now my dear fellow, he said to himself, we can take a stroll in the school yard, or perhaps we ought to go over to the secretary's office and see if there's a letter addressed to the *Herr Doktor*.

Rechnitz went to the office. He had not been there on the previous day, or indeed on the day before that, for he was not a great letter-hunter like some teachers, who were constantly in and out of the secretary's room, rummaging and staring through all the mail for an answer to the crucial question of whether or not a letter had come for them. Even now he would not have entered had he not been at a loss for something to do between lessons.

The secretary sat at his little desk, his nose buried in a ledger, a pen in his hand, pretending to ignore the not inconsiderable presence of Rechnitz. And Rechnitz, having time to spare, and having also forgotten what he had come for, forgot the secretary's existence, too. He looked at the pictures on the wall, and at the space between the pictures. The secretary glanced up, then down again at his ledger, where he continued with his writing. Doubtless, thought Rechnitz, the celebrity whose portrait hangs on the wall believed a stern unbending expression suited him best. If not, he wouldn't have pulled such a face. – As for you, sir, you whose name I'm afraid I've forgotten, what exactly was the impression you were trying to make?

The secretary raised his nose like a divining rod, and their eyes met.

"Is there a letter for me?" asked Rechnitz.

The secretary stared at him contemptuously. "When do letters come from the post office? In the morning or afternoon? Since letters come in the afternoon, what is the sense in asking for them before people have properly digested their breakfasts?"

"I rather thought there might have been a letter for me from yesterday."

"From *yesterday?*" exclaimed the secretary in a tone of amazement. "Do you mean to tell me that a ship put in yesterday? Let me tell you there was no ship, or at any rate, no ship that brought any mail. But perhaps, Dr. Rechnitz, you mean *inland* mail? If it was inland mail, that is of course another matter."

"Yes, yes," said Rechnitz, grateful that this pedantic master of logic had put the subject on a reasonable basis. "Yes, indeed, I meant a letter from within the country; for example, from Jaffa itself."

The secretary laid his hand on a pile of letters and said, "The inland mail has indeed arrived, but I must inform you, Dr. Rechnitz, that no letter has come for you. That is to say, no letter from within the country and none from Jaffa, which, as you may know, forms part of that country."

"Yes, yes, of course," Rechnitz replied.

Why do you keep yessing at me? thought the secretary to himself. If there's no letter for you, what's the sense in saying yes? A queer lot, these Germans. You can never get them out of the habit of conforming. And yesterday he took out some new girl from Austria, a Viennese she might well be, besides all the others. Now where did they go walking? By the sea. And what time did they choose to go walking? Just at the time when the sea turns cold and gives you a chill. A teacher with a cold! – *Well!* The secretary sneezed.

XVII

The school bell rang again. Rechnitz stirred. It was the break between lessons and he was still free; he walked over to the book room, known as the "nature room" because it contained a number of minerals, plants, and taxidermied animals and birds of the country.

The books were in a locked cabinet. He had no great desire to read, and certainly no desire to ask the secretary for the keys, so he stood and surveyed the stuffed creatures, which had been acquired from Ilyushin the taxidermist. These specimens are always a witness to Ilyushin's love for all living things; it was this love of his which gave them life even after their death. How beautiful, thought Rechnitz, is that swallow. She sits on her perch as if she were only dozing. When he went out he closed the door softly, as if he feared to wake the bird.

Finally he went back to the staff room. It was empty and the table was clear of rolls and cakes. Instead there were notebooks on it, and pamphlets and textbooks, including a new arithmetic manual. He picked this up and put it down, picked it up again and took a look inside, checked the figures given and wrote: "Duly checked and proved correct."

Again the bell rang, and Rechnitz murmured to himself that it was time to go. He passed a hand over his brow, as though to stimulate his memory. What do I want? he asked himself. But he had not found the reply by the time he was up on the platform facing the class.

Rechnitz raised his eyes and tried to keep them on his students. But his lids felt heavy and his knees were shaking. He crossed his legs, rubbed his eyes, and looked over the class again. The boys and girls sat in their usual rows; but above their heads a cloud seemed to hang, turning the class into something solid and opaque. Rechnitz began, "Boys and girls, yesterday we stopped at..." But he felt weak and wanted to cry. He closed his eyes and began again, "So yesterday..." The class could tell that their teacher's mind was far away, and everyone began to follow his or her private concerns. Rachel's brother took a novel out of his pocket, laid it on his knees and began to read. His neighbors to the right and left busied themselves drawing pictures. The girls were behaving even worse. Raya's sister folded a paper plane and sent it flying at the nose of Asnat's sister, while Asnat's sister in turn held a little mirror up toward the sun and blinded her companions with the reflected rays. Rechnitz could see what was going on and his eyes ached with sorrow. How could these pupils, whom he treated as friends, disgrace him so?

"What are you reading over there?" he called out sharply.

Heilperin calmly exhibited his book and answered, *Sanin.*

"What's that?"

"A novel."

"And what's it about?"

"I don't know, sir. I haven't read it yet."

"You don't know! You don't know anything, do you? – And you, what are *you* up to there?"

The boy trembled and pushed his notebook away.

"What's your opinion?" said Rechnitz. "Would you say it's worth my while to see what you have been drawing? Not worth my while? If so, why waste time on a thing that's not worth doing? As for you, my little friend, my dear Miss Magargot, if I had such a delightful mirror as yours, I should hold it up to your face and see two hard-working students instead of one. Yes, my friends, I suppose I *am* being sarcastic, and that's not what I am here for. But my dear friends, you're not here either just to read novels. Very soon Yehia will be ringing his bell and we shall be going home. What we shall do at home is a problem; because once a person doesn't do what he has to do, he doesn't know anymore what to do instead. And now Yehia, God bless him, is sounding the bell. So goodbye, boys and girls. Goodbye."

XVIII

What shall I do now? Rechnitz wondered. I can't go to the Consul's, because lunch time is near and I haven't been invited to lunch. If I went, Shoshanah would think I was behaving as if I owned her and had the right to turn up whenever I liked. No, it's no good, he thought. It was half past twelve. In half an hour the restaurant would be full of regular customers; if he didn't hurry there would be no lunch left. He had not eaten there for two days and the proprietress would assume he was not coming.

Suddenly he remembered what he had been trying to recall in the break before his second lesson. Tonight, or last night, or even the night before, he had been invited to Shoshanah's for dinner. Her room was small and pleasant. The table was set for a meal with bread and *matzah*, butter and milk, tomatoes and cucumbers, eggs and cheese. In the middle of the table stood a bowl of strawberries and on the strawberries was a red dusting of sugar. The room had a pleasant scent, and not only because of the strawberries: when Shoshanah went out to bring in the tea, he looked at the wardrobe where she kept her clothes and saw a bunch of roses on top. He counted twelve roses, and was pleased, although he was not superstitious, to find that they did not add up to thirteen. What did they talk about, he and Shoshanah? They talked about all sorts of people, including her father, the Consul. Oddly enough, Shoshanah referred to him as if he were Jacob's father and not her own. And when she mentioned him she said,

"Of course, I don't know him well, but I would suppose…" whatever it was she attributed to him. Jacob ate very little, and for that reason Shoshanah refrained from taking much. Although he knew that she ought to eat more, still he did not force his appetite. After they had eaten and drunk, she went and sat down on the sofa and he sat on a chair facing her. She showed him a more comfortable place, saying, "Sit here," but he did not leave his chair, although he was feeling a pain in his shoulders from sitting where he was. In order not to tire Shoshanah, he resolved to leave at nine o'clock. The time came, but he still stayed. They sat talking about Rachel and Leah, and about Frau Ehrlich, Shoshanah's mother. And this too was strange, that Shoshanah did not know where her mother was born until he told her. He glanced at his watch and found it was nearly ten. Time to leave, he told her; but Shoshanah answered that it wasn't yet nine o'clock. "It's already ten," he said. "Is it really?" said Shoshanah in surprise, and she adjusted her watch. After a while he got up to leave and Shoshanah went out to accompany him. When they had gone halfway, he wanted to turn back and see her home, but she would not allow this. She made her way home, while he waited for his streetcar. He bought a ticket and climbed in. The streetcar filled up and started to move. On its way it kept stopping to take on more and more passengers. Two young fellows got in and one sat on the other's knees. He heard them talking to one another about Otto Weininger and his book *Sex and Character*. The journey continued for an hour. And then, oddly enough, Jacob had found himself again sitting with Shoshanah; and it was not yet eleven o'clock, although he had left Shoshanah's house at ten, and she had accompanied him halfway, and he had even traveled for an hour on the streetcar, and spent an hour at home. How could it be, then, that he was with Shoshanah at nearly eleven o'clock?

XIX

After his meal Rechnitz didn't linger in the little restaurant and didn't go back to his room. His habits had changed since the day of the Consul's arrival in Jaffa; the times when he used to relax over lunch, make his own coffee and read a book, seemed part of prehistory. He said to himself: The Consul will be taking his afternoon nap now.

Shoshanah will be sitting in her room arranging her photographs. If that's where she is, I can take a walk in front of the hotel; and if she is out in the garden, I can walk there, as I did the day before yesterday. But the day before yesterday I was with others, and today I shall be walking alone. That stroll with Rachel and Leah on the day of Shoshanah's arrival had given him a certain self-confidence in her presence, not because the stroll had made her jealous but for another reason, which was actually the same reason; it showed that Jacob Rechnitz was not isolated from the world and also that she, Shoshanah Ehrlich, was by no means the only woman in that world. In fact he had not intended to take a walk that day, either with Rachel or with Leah, still less with both of them at once; it just happened that Leah had come across him. And so on, and so on. Yet if one looked more deeply into the matter, it seemed that there was another truth here; namely, that Rechnitz was quite in the habit of taking some girl out for a walk, whether her name were Rachel or Leah, or indeed Asnat or Raya or Mira or Tamara.

It is the way of people who have grown up in a beautiful place to take its charms for granted. But when they visit another lovely town, they not only note the new charms, but first become aware of the beauty they have always lived with. So for Rechnitz, the arrival of Shoshanah in Jaffa served also to reveal the beauty of the girls with whom he was already familiar.

We have spoken of Leah Luria and Rachel Heil-perin. Friends as they were, Rachel was the more sharp-witted and Leah the more sympathetic. Leah was older than any of her friends and yet her eyes shone with youth and good nature, as if they were the dwelling place of angels. If her talk was not too solid, still it gladdened the heart. When they were out on an excursion and sat down to rest, it was Leah who would arrange a meal for the whole group, seeing that everyone got his share and forgetting to look after her own needs in her concern for the welfare of others. As for Rachel, she was not to be measured by any standards of good or evil. If she did something wrong, you could not be angry with her; if she did a good deed, she did not think well of herself for it. She was also the kind of person you could speak to without any pretense. Yet this merit was also a defect, for nothing you did could help you, since all depended on her and nothing on you yourself.

And now let us consider Asnat Magargot. She came from Kirov, and it was said that her father had gone bankrupt and absconded to the Land of Israel, much as most persons in that condition abscond to America. Bankruptcy and embezzlement are great transgressions, which cannot be atoned for until the ill-gotten gains are restored to their rightful owners, and even then it is doubtful if one is completely absolved. Magargot, however, was not very guilt-stricken; rather, he behaved as if he had done a great favor to the Land of Israel, proving by his action that the Settlement was a practical proposition, and that sudden departures from Europe need not have America for their destination.

Asnat, like Leah Luria and Rachel Heilperin, was a tall girl. She wore a greenish brown dress of fine smooth weave, with a silver belt whose roped ends fell below her knees. Though her dress was like the habit of a monk, Asnat's lips were eager – but not for kisses. You might be sitting beside her for two or three hours, my dear friend, almost crazy with the desire to take her in your arms; and she too might share something of the same idea. But that was all. You would merely pick up the two tassels that fell from her belt and go on talking about Ibsen's plays or something of the sort. The world has its set ways, and if it occurred to you to deviate from them, you would find this impossible with Asnat. Her steel-blue eyes cut your soul into little pieces. This was the more surprising because the kind of topics Asnat discussed – all those "problems of modern life" – were just the kind that create the greatest intimacy; and yet you could not so much as touch her with your little finger. What then did Asnat really want? She wanted much, and she wanted nothing; she wanted nothing, and she wanted much. On a summer night she would take a fancy to walking as far as Rishon LeZion and ask you to escort her. And you would walk along with her by the sand dunes for three hours in the darkness, going by night and coming back by night, without her letting you touch even the tassels of her belt, either on the way out or on the way back.

Raya Zablodovsky was a relative of Asnat, though you could hardly find two girls so unlike, either in stature or feature. Asnat was tall and her face bore witness to a quick wit; Raya was no taller than a child and her face testified neither to a quick wit, nor even to a slow-paced one. She had sandy hair and her lips pouted as if she had just tasted an unripe fruit. In disposition she was withdrawn, like a bird that covers its head with its wings. Some of her friends declared her too egotistical, others even thought her malicious. Yet they could not help being drawn to her, since both qualities, that is to say both the self-love and the malice, were cloaked in a humor that never failed to surprise. Thus, she might decide to seat herself on a boulder after spreading some fine silk scarf over it; if you remarked that this was strange behavior, she would say, "Not at all. It isn't my scarf, you see." Never in her life had Raya read a book cover to cover, neither in Russian nor in Hebrew, not even the books that everyone was talking about. She failed her examinations twice and left school before finishing, without any regrets. "In the end," she would say, "you forget everything you have learned. As for me, I forget without bothering to learn it first." How, then, did she come to be one of the girls in Rechnitz's group? Simply because this is life's way: once you belong to a certain group, you belong, however different you are.

Raya's neighbor was Mira Vorbzhitsky, the daughter of Niuma Vorbzhitsky, who had been a guard of the Sharon settlements. He was the terror of bandits, and if he found any within his beat he was capable of picking a man up and using him as a flail against his companions like someone beating a garment with a stick. Mira had more agility than any girl in Jaffa, not excepting even Rachel Heilperin, for when she was little her father used to make her ride an unsaddled horse which he would set galloping over the hills, paying no heed to her frightened cries. She was still accustomed to riding bareback, and on occasion she would take a horse from between the shafts of a carriage and mount it and ride as far as Sarona. Although she had the graceful figure of a girl, she resembled a handsome youth. When she was a child and her father was still a guard, they had lived on the outskirts of the village away from other settlers, where her mother used to dress her in boys' clothes as a precaution against the Arabs. Her bearing still had something boyish about it, though her manners were those of a girl, and she was dear to her companions of both sexes.

Something has yet to be said about Tamara Levi. Her father had been a doctor. Once in the rainy season, on a dark overcast night, he was out riding on his donkey to visit a patient in the settlements. The donkey stumbled into a flooded wadi, and the doctor drowned. Tamara lived with her mother in a single room in a large courtyard of many apartments. The mother was a rabbi's daughter and well aware of her standing, but she found it difficult to earn a livelihood. She would care for the sick, sometimes sitting with them all night. Her husband had left her nothing when he died; and now she had to make a living for herself and Tamara and to see that her daughter had the same education as other girls of good family. Mother and daughter loved each other much, but this involved them in serious conflict. For it happened that a certain school Secretary, with quite a good income, was courting Tamara and her mother approved of the match. As for Tamara herself, she said that she had no objection to marriage but that she did not see why it should be with this man in particular, even though he did have a good position at the school where Rechnitz taught.

Tamara's hair, one supposes, was ash-grey; her eyes, it may be assumed, were blue; but the blue-tinted radiance that lit up her features and dazzled the eyes made these two colors seem interchangeable. At first sight she might have escaped your notice. Later, if not for the narcissus or carnation pinned on her breast, you might miss the presence of a heart underneath. Her real name was Tamar but she liked to be called Tamara, and since she was such a dear child, let us call her by the name she preferred. Her conversation was not notably wise; if one cared to say so, it even tended to silliness; but her lips caressed your heart much as the red flower on her own heart was caressed by the tip of her nose. One time Rechnitz had set his lips to hers; they had quivered slightly and just touched his in return. A touch that was hardly a touch at all. Heavens above, if that was the shadow of a kiss, what would a true kiss be like? No girl in the world had such lips as hers, and, besides this, every touch of her hand was like a kiss. But was there any man in Jaffa who knew it?

Tamara had this virtue too: she never used to complain or seem angry. She would look up at you admiringly and accept whatever you said as a gift of grace. So you would sit contentedly surveying the tip of her nose and letting the radiance of her face wrap you in a sweet blue mist. Only once had Rechnitz kissed Tamara and he did not repeat the performance; he was, after all, her teacher, and it was not proper for teachers to kiss their pupils. This applied even though there were teachers who permitted themselves such conduct and even though Tamara had now left school and belonged to his group of friends. At times Rechnitz regretted the kiss; at other times he regretted not having made a second attempt. However that may be, it was a good thing that he had no occasion to be alone with her, for more reasons than one. Since the school Secretary had his eye on her with a view to marriage, it would not have been decent to spoil someone's life for the sake of a fleeting pleasure. That was a sufficient reason, but there was still another one which Jacob buried in his heart.

XX

A strange shriek interrupted the train of Rechnitz's thoughts. The parrot, which on the evening before last had perched in his cage at the hotel imitating the jackals' screams, was now in the garden answering the sound of the striking clock. Before him stood the old Baron, dressed in white, with a tropical sun-helmet on his head. The Baron was holding out an apple and the parrot, standing on one leg, extended the other, snatched the apple and pecked at it. "*Schmeckt's, Herrchen? – Tasty for you sir?*" the Baron asked. The parrot shook his hooked beak and cried, "*Schmeckt, Herrchen!*"

"A fine bird," said the Baron to Rechnitz. "I bought it from a hunter who had caught it to eat. There are places, you know, where they eat parrot meat. "*Verflucht! Dammit!*" he called to the parrot.

"*Verflucht!*" it answered back.

The Baron laughed and wagged his finger at the bird.

"*Verflucht,*" he said to it, "Dammit, bird, you mustn't curse!"

The parrot replied with a shriek, "*Verflucht! Verflucht! Dammit! Dammit!*"

When Rechnitz had disengaged himself from the Baron, he went on to the hotel. By now, he reflected, the Consul will have awakened from his nap and lit the cigar he smokes out of boredom. I shall go across to him, perhaps he will be grateful to me for rescuing him from his boredom. And what will Shoshanah have to say? She will say nothing be-cause that is her way. There are some people whose silences are awesome; we imagine their minds to be full of great thoughts beyond our ken, thoughts which keep them from communicating, and this makes us shrink in their presence, believing that they hold in their hands the keys of all wisdom. Yet if we consider the matter well, we shall find that their silence grows out of overweening pride and that they don't surpass us by so much as the breadth of a parrot's claw. It is only because we shrink that they tower above us. And why do we thus belittle ourselves before them? This calls for investigation but I have no time for it. It is after four o'clock, the Consul is already up and having his boredom. I have extended my reflections too far and extended monologues are to be avoided in modern drama. *Verflucht!* I like the smell of baking in butter over there. Yehia's wife does all her baking in oil because the Jews here don't have any butter and because people in the East prefer olive oil to dairy products anyhow. It isn't a thing you can reason about but simply a matter of taste, just as the Sefardi teacher will say "a quarter-hour" instead of "a quarter of an hour." And now a quarter of an hour has gone by and I am still standing outside, delivering long monologues.

Rechnitz entered the hotel. Nobody was in the lobby, except the waiters setting the tables and brewing coffee. He walked through, glancing from side to side. The absent guests, he thought, the honored guests, are still sitting in their private rooms waiting patiently until the mere nobodies have prepared their food and drink. As for me, I'm one of the nobodies; and if I haven't the ability to prepare meals and drinks, at least the gods have given me the power to save somebody from boredom. "*Schmeckt's, Herrchen?*" he asked himself and looked around again. The hotel clerk saw Rechnitz and said, "There's a letter for you, sir."

"A letter?" Rechnitz stammered, and his heart began to pound. The clerk brought the letter; Rechnitz took it and went outside. He walked through the garden, stopped under a tree, and leaned against it with the letter in his hand. A letter from Shoshanah? Let's see what Shoshanah has to tell me. Let's open the letter and see. But when he opened it he saw it was not from Shoshanah but from her father. Again his heart began to beat fast, not the rapid heartbeat of a man awaiting some happy event, but such as one feels when expecting disaster.

Again he looked round. Seeing that no one was about, he reflected: Shoshanah has told her father all that happened by the sea and he must be punishing me with a reprimand. Rechnitz was filled with rage. Does that old man think because he has thrown me a few crumbs from his table that he has the right to abuse me? Keep your crumbs, old man, for the dogs. I can provide for myself and, as for my name in the world of science, I don't owe it to you. *Verflucht,* these people with money! If you have taken the least scrap from them, they think they have bought you. I don't mind thanking you, Consul, for all you have done on my behalf, but you have not bought my soul. And if your daughter should be pleased to follow me, I shall take her from under your nose.

While he was saying this to himself, he looked at the words of the letter, and as he looked his eyes lit up. Here was no rebuke but instead a kind of apology. The Consul and his daughter had departed for Jerusalem without managing to take leave of him in advance. He saw too that the Consul sent his best greetings, as well as his regards, and added: "As soon as we are back in Jaffa, we shall be delighted to see you."

It was a good thing that Rechnitz read that letter. Even as he did so he put all the bitterness out of his heart. His soul returned and he reflected: All my life I never aspired to Shoshanah. When I used to speak about her to her father it was with humility, and suddenly I've grown bold. If I were now to go to him and demand his daughter, he would be shocked. No, I shall not argue or pick a quarrel or talk big, but act modestly until he sees and understands for himself how much I love Shoshanah. And if she is indeed to be my partner for life, as she pledged to be, I shall wait patiently for good angels to spread their wings over us and make our wedding canopy.

As he reflected, Rechnitz felt a lighter, calmer spirit. It is best for a man to act in character. What nonsense to think I had it in me to carry off Shoshanah against her father's will – as if I had the power to do any such thing! At that moment Rechnitz saw himself as a man who has gone after an enemy, only to find that very enemy his friend. His humility gave him strength. He looked into himself and said, That is how I have been all my days and that is how I have come through. And so I shall be all my days and so continue to come through.

XXI

Herr Ehrlich stayed in Jerusalem longer than he had intended. The anniversary of his wife's death came around while he was there and he wanted to commemorate it in the Holy City. The day passed fittingly: he said Kaddish at the Western Wall, gave alms to the poor and visited various houses of charity. Certain things he saw met with his approval and he took due note of them. As for the rest, he looked the other way and ignored shortcomings, being mindful of the city and the occasion. He also paid a visit to the Sha'arei Zedek Hospital, where he made the acquaintance of a certain doctor who sacrificed his sleep for the sake of his patients, not laying his head upon a pillow unless it were on a Sabbath or festival night and taking no payment beyond his simple needs. When Herr Ehrlich saw plaques affixed to the walls of the hospital and on each plaque the name of some benefactor who had contributed to the cost of the building or the care of the sick, he too made a contribution for the upkeep of a bed, to grace his wife's soul and serve as a lasting memorial in Jerusalem.

The Consul was very pleased with the city. True, what he had seen with his own eyes was unlike the Jerusalem of legend or the Jerusalem of his imagination. There were many things that could well have been dispensed with and also many things lacking that might well have been there. But since one did not really know where to make a start, or how to proceed in the way of reform, it was best to leave Jerusalem as she was.

Once again, Rechnitz is seated facing the Consul in the Jaffa hotel. The weather is chilly, the air damp; hot embers glow in the copper tray before them. The Consul has a thick cigar in his mouth and a woolen rug rests on his knees. He warms his hands alternately with the cigar and over the hot coals. Shoshanah is some distance away, wrapped in her beaver coat. The coals whisper to themselves and the tray, reflecting their red glow, whispers back. The room grows warmer, the air more heated; a sweet languor seeps into the spoken word, like the languor that surrounds the body. From the sea outside the sound of waves mounts like the distant roaring of beasts of prey. The Consul shakes the ash from his cigar and remarks, "Today it's impossible to take a walk on the beach." And Rechnitz blushes; can the Consul be alluding to the walk he had taken with Shoshanah?

But in fact the Consul was only referring to the stormy weather that had delayed his departure. What is more, he was glad that he did not have to travel, after wandering from country to country for over a year. He had seen so many lands: more than he could number, more names than he could remember. If he had not listed in his notebook the name of each place visited he would never have known where he had or had not been. Shoshanah too was glad of the delay. She had taken many photographs and collected many souvenirs and now she needed time to arrange them.

On the day of her return from Jerusalem Shoshanah had been very fatigued. Without finishing her meal she had left for her room and gone to bed. But on the next night she lingered over dinner. Unasked, quite of her own accord, she brought an album of her photographs and souvenirs to show to Jacob. She was astonished at the way he recognized each object and gave it its proper name, and even happier at the serious interest he took in her collection. And because she was grateful, she wanted to repay him by recounting various stories. That night, Shoshanah told Jacob many tales. This was one of them: "Once upon a time there was a king who wished to marry me. This king had a fine palace made of palm fronds, and he also had two wives. One of these wives wore sardine tins in her earlobes to enhance her beauty; the other one looked just like the girl you were walking with on the day I arrived in Jaffa. But," added Shoshanah, "you were out with two girls together and as I don't know which is which, I can't tell you which one looks like the king's wife."

The Consul laughed and cried in surprise, "What? Do you take girls out for walks? I thought scientists were completely wrapped up in their work! It looks as though science is a complacent mistress who doesn't object to rivals. Tell me, Shoshanah, are they pretty, these two girls?"

Shoshanah looked at Jacob and answered, "That is for you to say."

"If," said her father, "he is thinking of his own reputation, he will answer that they are extremely beautiful; if he is thinking of yours, he will say they are not at all attractive. And so, my dear daughter, *you* tell me – are they good-looking?"

Shoshanah replied, "Whatever I may say, Dr. Rechnitz thinks they are."

"How do you know that?" asked the Consul.

"If it were not so, he would not have brought them along to exhibit to me."

"I did *not* bring them along to exhibit to you," Rechnitz protested.

"No?"

"No! It was like this, really. That afternoon after leaving here, I just happened to see them on my way and we took a walk together. And since I was invited to dinner and didn't know when it would be served, I went to ask the waiter, and they were good enough to come along with me."

"And the flowers you presented to me," said Shoshanah, "were they given to you by one of them, or by both?"

"What you say is partly true," Jacob answered. "They both put themselves out to bring you flowers, but those I actually brought to you came from the gardener."

"They assumed," said Shoshanah, "that I would be here today and gone tomorrow?"

"Quite possibly."

"But if so, they were wrong."

"Wrong indeed," answered Jacob, and he did not know whether to be glad or not.

Shoshanah added, "Father intends to spend the whole winter here – don't you, Papa?"

The Consul, questioning, looked at his daughter, then nodded his head in agreement.

"Yes, daughter, I've been weighing whether it isn't worth my while to spend the winter here. You people don't realize how hard the

European winter is, and all the harder now that I'm used to warm countries."

Shoshanah stood up from the table, took her father's head in both hands and kissed his forehead. "Good Papa!" There were tears in her father's eyes.

XXII

That afternoon Rechnitz went to the post office and came across Shoshanah walking about the market place. Her arms were filled with pottery. It was Shoshanah's way to buy local wares at every place she visited, and here in Jaffa she had purchased various pitchers and clay vessels. What would she do with them? She might take a few with her or she might leave them all behind at the hotel, for next day, no doubt, she would find something more pleasing.

"May I help you?" Jacob asked her.

Shoshanah glanced at him for a moment and held out two pitchers. "Don't worry about them too much; if they get broken, they get broken – the market's full of them."

"If that's the case, then give me more," said Jacob. "I'll be careful not to break them."

They left the market together by carriage. Shoshanah said, "I always believed carriages were only invented to get in my way when walking, but all of a sudden you have put me into one and I find I am no longer afraid of horses and vehicles. Why do you look surprised?"

"I certainly am surprised. You are so used to traveling, yet you talk of carriages getting in your way."

Shoshanah said, "I'm used to long journeys and forget that even short distances can be made easier with conveyances."

"Yet you seem more tired by these short distances than by long journeys."

"Great things add greatly to one's strength," she said. "Oh, how beautiful those palms are! How many are there? Eight, nine?"

"Yes, nine," Jacob answered.

"I have never in my life seen such beautiful palm trees."

He wanted to say that he himself had already shown them to her but thought better of it and remarked, "Surely you have seen finer ones in the tropics?"

"Finer ones? Never in my life," she repeated. "Driver, stop a moment. I don't know what has come over me, I could swear I have seen them before! No, not in a dream, Jacob, but awake!"

She blushed as she spoke; then, telling the driver to proceed, she said no more until they arrived at the hotel.

When the carriage came to a stop, she said to Jacob, "If you don't mind, let's go into the garden. Tell the driver he can leave the pots in the hotel. What language were you speaking to him? Hebrew, was it? And isn't Hebrew the language of the prayer book? So this driver speaks like the prayers; and you too, Jacob. How wonderful you all are here! Let's sit on this bench. I knew, Jacob, that you would agree with me. What a lot of good turns you have done me today. You have carried my pottery for me, and put me in a carriage, and brought me all the way back. It's good for a person to be good. We too ought to be good, not wicked. Do you think I am a wicked person? Sometimes I think so myself but it's not really true, I'm just too lazy to get people out of the notion of my wickedness."

Jacob said, "It would never occur to anyone to call you wicked."

"It may never have occurred to you, but how do you know what others think?"

"I judge the rest of the world by myself."

"But isn't it a kind of sinful pride to measure all mankind by your own standard?"

"On the contrary," said Jacob, "it's a virtue, because by so doing I can correct any mistaken ideas of yours."

"Please tell me, Jacob, what have human beings to be proud about?"

"You speak just like your father. He asks what have human beings to dispute about."

"I have never disputed with anybody in my life," said Shoshanah.

"You have no need to, since everyone rushes to do your bidding."

"Everyone, that is, except myself. I sometimes think I have no will at all and whatever I do is done without any good reason. I am more frivolous than a child who makes his decisions by flipping a coin. What does a girl like me want?"

The waitress set up a little table and asked, "What would the lady like me to bring?"

"I don't want anything," said Shoshanah.

"You see, Shoshanah," Jacob remarked, "you have a very strong will. Since you didn't want anything, you said just that."

Shoshanah blushed. "I really deserve to be scolded; it didn't occur to me that *you* might like something. But you don't? Well then, let's just sit and talk."

This was the most delightful meeting Jacob had known with Shoshanah since the day she came to Jaffa. It had about it something new and something old and familiar; new, because she had not previously sat with him in this garden, and old, too, because it was thus in their childhood that they had sat together in that other garden of her father. The good gods give us more than we deserve. Here are Jacob and Shoshanah among green boughs, and in winter time, when the garden of their childhood is covered with snow and the pond overlaid with ice. They talk about themselves and the world outside, which is no more than a small part of their own. At times, the good gods deal well with mortals, allowing them to see eternity in an hour. Let us then ask the gods to prolong this hour without end or limit.

Shoshanah had laid her fine, delicate hands before her on the table. Jacob gazed at them, as he used to gaze at her mother's hands when she would place them on the table and his lips would long to touch them. We are so made that our memories lead from one thing to another; sometimes these lie close together, sometimes far apart. Jacob now recalled a time when he happened to be at Ein Rogel, at Ilyushin's, when he was stretching an animal skin on a board; he had spread his hands out like that, or almost like that, in the course of his work. As Jacob sat there, surprised at the direction his thoughts had taken, the parrot suddenly made himself heard, crying out, "*Verflucht!*"

Shoshanah shuddered and looked around her. Jacob laughed. "It's only the parrot," he said.

"Just this very moment," he went on, "I was thinking about a taxidermist I know called Ilyushin. I wouldn't say that bird is a mind reader, but all the same it's very queer – just at the moment when I thought of Ilyushin, the parrot called *Verflucht.*

"Illusion?"

"Yes, Ilyushin."

Shoshanah said, "Yesterday evening you remarked that you changed the flowers your girlfriends gave you to bring me. What was the point in changing them?"

Jacob's cheeks flushed but Shoshanah did not notice.

She had closed her eyes, as she had a way of doing sometimes in the course of conversation.

"What was the point?" he repeated.

Shoshanah nodded, her eyes still closed.

"I changed them because I'd found nicer ones."

"That sounds plausible," said Shoshanah. "Now tell me the real reason. Oh, I can see that just now you don't know; perhaps another time you will. What was the name of the taxidermist at Ein Rogel?"

"His name was Ilyushin."

Shoshanah opened her eyes. "That's it – Illusion."

"And what has Ilyushin to do with us?" asked Jacob.

"Since you mentioned him, I wanted to know what he was called. Now that I know, you don't have to say any more about him. Cattle and wild beasts may enjoy a privilege granted to no man except the mummies in Egypt. Don't you smoke? I'll call a waiter to bring you some cigarettes. Let's honor the wisdom of Egypt, the land that gave eternal life to her sons, by ordering Egyptian cigarettes."

Then, forgetting all about the cigarettes, Shoshanah went on, "Our days on earth are like a shadow, and the time of our affliction is the length of our days. How fortunate are those mummies, laid in the ground and freed from all trouble and toil. If I could only be like one of them!" Shoshanah opened her eyes and looked up as if longing for release from the afflictions of the world.

"From the day of your mother's funeral, I have not seen you," Jacob said. "And even on that day I didn't really see you. You seemed so distant from this world, Shoshanah."

"No, Jacob, I felt as if the world were distant from me. And now, here I am, still not part of the world."

"And in all those years, have you really had no happiness?"

Shoshanah neither spoke nor moved. Looking across at her, Rechnitz took in her sadness. He wanted to speak but could not find words. Hesitantly, he said, "You are so troubled, Shoshanah. What is it?"

She stirred a little. "What were you asking, Jacob?"

"I was asking what is it that makes you so sad?"

Shoshanah smiled. "You ask, 'What is it?' as if there were one reason alone. There are many, and each is enough to make one sad, very sad indeed."

"But why?"

"I don't know—" she stopped short and remained very still.

"And yet you are, both of us are, young enough, with all our life before us."

"But that life before us, do you think it's going to be any better than the life that lies behind?"

"I haven't thought much about that," said Jacob.

"Neither have I," said Shoshanah.

"Then what grounds have you for saying what you did?"

"What did I say?"

"You know what you said."

"Just idle talk," said Shoshanah.

And Jacob too felt melancholy. This is the girl who wants to be my wife, he reflected. He felt restive as he considered her. This girl wants me to marry her, he thought again. And even while he pondered, he realized that without her the whole world would be lost to him.

The sound of voices startled Jacob. "People are coming!" Shoshanah nodded and replied, "It's Papa with the old Baron." As they approached, the Consul broke into a ribald laugh. Apparently the old man had just told him an off-color story. The laughter struck Jacob's ears unpleasantly; he had always known the Consul as a serious-minded man, yet here he was behaving frivolously. Shoshanah stood up and said, "Let's go."

They walked away together. A little girl came by with a basket in her hand. Jacob turned to her. "What are you doing here?" he said. The little girl answered, "My Mommy sent me to get some lemons." He bent down and swung her in the air. "Sweetheart, I'd love to carry you off. You and your basket together. Tell me, what would your Mommy say if I carried you away?" The child answered solemnly, "Mommy wouldn't like it." Jacob laughed. "Tell your mother that you're a clever little girl." "Yes, I'll tell her," she replied.

"Whose charming child is that?" asked Shoshanah.

"She's the sister of a girl I teach."

"One of those you were walking with here in the garden?"

Jacob hesitated a little. "You saw those two girls; how did they strike you?"

"They're very lovely," said Shoshanah.

"Does that mean that you approve of them?"

"If you think well of them," replied Shoshanah, "so do I."

"I don't know how to take that."

"I mean just what I said. But you have other friends besides, haven't you? Tell me about them."

Jacob began to tell her. When he had got round to describing Tamara, Shoshanah looked at him rather closely.

The two old men were coming back, the Baron laughing raucously. This time, it would seem, the Consul had capped his story with a spicier one.

"So you're here, you two?" said the Consul.

"Yes," answered Shoshanah, and went on to praise Jacob for his kindness in calling a carriage and bringing her back to the hotel.

"Happy is he who finds a good escort," said the Baron, and he cast a benevolent glance on Jacob.

"But aren't you cold, Shoshanah?" asked the Consul.

"No, I'm neither too cold nor too warm. I'm quite happy, Papa."

The Consul looked at his daughter for a moment and went off with the Baron. At Shoshanah's suggestion, she and Jacob sat down again together.

"Once," said Shoshanah, "I dreamed that I was dead. I wasn't happy, I wasn't sad, but my body felt such rest as no one knows in the land of the living. And this was the best of it, that I wanted nothing, I asked for nothing, it just felt as if I were disappearing into blue distances that would never end. Next morning I opened a book and read in it that nobody dreams of himself as dead. If that's so, perhaps it was not a dream but wide-awake reality. But then, how can I be alive after my death? It's a puzzle to me, Jacob. Do you believe in the resurrection of the dead?"

"No, certainly not," Jacob said.

"Don't say 'certainly.' These certainties of yours bring me to tears." As she spoke, she closed her eyes.

At that moment, Shoshanah seemed to hover over those blue distances she had spoken of. Then suddenly she answered Jacob's gaze. She took out her handkerchief, wiped her eyes, opened them and looked at him with absolute love. After a while, she said, "I am going to close my eyes and you, Jacob, are to kiss me on the eyelids."

Jacob's own eyes filled with tears. With the tears still there, he placed his lips on her wet lashes.

XXIII

Everything good happens when your attention is turned the other way. So it was with Rechnitz. An elderly scholar in New York, with whom Rechnitz had exchanged specimens of seaweed, had suggested the creation of an academic chair for him; the suggestion had been taken up and now Rechnitz received a written offer. Even though he had already won himself a high reputation, Rechnitz had not expected anything like this, for he was still a young man and aware that he had many superiors in the field.

He was lying on his couch that morning mid-way between sleep and waking. His thoughts went off in various directions without his knowing where they were heading. There are times when a man's limbs are still and his mind is at rest, and there are times when his mind goes wandering and carries back many thoughts. There are times when the limbs are still but find no rest or the mind goes wandering but carries back no thought and no idea. Yet again, both states may exist together: the mind goes wandering and the limbs are still, and a man finds neither rest in his limbs nor thought in his mind. Rechnitz wanted to get up from his couch but knew it would be useless. And so he had yielded to this kind of lethargy that brings no benefit, when he heard someone knocking on his door. He jumped up, opened the door, and there was the postman with a letter. Rechnitz received it with a groan, as if he had been interrupted in some important undertaking. The postman slung his bag over his shoulder and went away; Rechnitz opened his letter and read it. Certainly this was good news, and would have been so even if he had been expecting the appointment. All the more so when it came as a surprise.

Rechnitz always offered thanks for any benefits that came his way, sometimes to the good gods, sometimes to the Only One. Now he was silent and said no prayer, but whatever it was that had dulled his mind before now passed away completely.

He dressed and went to call on someone whose English was better than his. Actually there was no need, since he already knew what the letter was about. Nor did this man tell him anything new. But his eyes widened with surprise and he reached out his hand to Rechnitz, saying, "Congratulations, Professor!"

Perhaps Rechnitz was more moved by this response than he had been by the occasion for it. Possibly, too, the man he consulted was more excited about the news than Rechnitz himself. Before the day was out all Jaffa knew that a young fellow who taught at the school had gained an unheard of distinction. For in those days honor paid to learning still counted among ordinary people; all the more so when the honor carried with it a good salary. How many scholars were there who didn't even get as far as a university post, and here was an ordinary young teacher promoted to be a full professor!

In Rechnitz's time, a number of scholars had already settled in the Land of Israel. Of these, some were engaged in research in Palestinology, others in biblical studies. They had this in common: they made their studies an adjunct to interests outside the field of pure scientific learning, such as national, religious or social causes. Some of them were internationally famous and their opinions were generally accepted until the intellectual climate changed and new scholars came to the fore. As for Rechnitz, he subordinated his work to no other consideration. He took trouble and pains solely in the cause of pure knowledge. All seasons were the same to him. A storm outside or blazing sunshine never kept him back. Besides collecting marine plants from the sea off Jaffa, he collected them, too, off the coasts of Haifa, off Acre, Hadera and Caesarea, since the plants in the sea around Jaffa differ from those in other regions. And here we must remember that Rechnitz had found no professional colleague in the country and did his work in solitude. This isolation, which may lead to slackness, can prove a blessing to the true scholar, for if he makes some new discovery he clarifies its meaning all to himself and does not waste his time in superfluous discussions. With the vigor of youth, with keen intellect and a discriminating eye, Rechnitz studied, investigated and assembled minute details as well as general principles, constructing from these a complete system. This ability to see and observe was matched by his ability to set out his observations in writing. His "Remarks on the Nature of Cyrenean Seaweeds," and even more so, those on Cerulean Seaweeds, made his reputation. And at the conference of zoologists and botanists, most of the lecturers referred to him; even those who disagreed with his views accorded him high praise.

Jaffa was getting more and more excited over the affair. People who had nothing to do with universities were talking about this young Ph.D. who had been appointed a professor. Everyone who came across Rechnitz, whether an acquaintance of his or not, would stop to congratulate him. His actual acquaintances invited him to take a drink in honor of the occasion, and wherever he went he found a holiday spread awaiting him. Here too we should remark that whatever people did was done in honor of science, for the parents of daughters knew well that now Rechnitz was a professor the Consul would never let go of him.

What is more, the daughters themselves knew that from the day of Shoshanah Ehrlich's arrival in Jaffa, Rechnitz had made himself scarce, especially now that he was getting ready to leave. Nevertheless, they retained their affection for him. Leah sent him more flowers of the kind she had given him for the Ehrlich girl on that first day. Tamara baked a cake for him in the shape of a boat and set on it a little American flag made of sugar. Even Rachel Heilperin put herself out so far as to write him a letter of congratulation; and this was no small matter, for although she could speak with much fluency, when she sat down to write she got stuck on the very first phrase. Should one write "My dear sir," or "Dear Dr. Rechnitz," or "My very dear friend Mr. Rechnitz"?

As for Rechnitz, the expression of people's good wishes moved him deeply. Imagine, even the school Secretary, who had seemed to bear a grudge against him, was as pleased at this success as if it had been his own. Needless to say, Rechnitz's colleagues at school were delighted. In a sense they were happy for his sake, in a sense for their own; for here was one of their number, a fellow-teacher, who had gained this honor, so that it became theirs as well. And what an honor! From the time of Nietzsche until the time of Rechnitz, no young man in such a position had been appointed professor.

For the most part, Rechnitz left matters concerning his new appointment for time to settle. He returned to his normal life as though nothing had happened, except that now he began to learn English and to occupy himself with some matters which previously would not have received much attention.

XXIV

Rechnitz could see that Shoshanah's father knew what had passed between the two of them. A girl like Shoshanah was not used to concealing her actions. But it was doubtful whether her father knew just how things stood, since Shoshanah's outlook was different from his own and she would certainly see the situation not as it was but as her heart pictured it. Even if she had told her father all, it was unlikely that he grasped the root of the matter. However that may have been, Jacob did not find a suitable pretext for speaking to him about what had happened, and he regretted this and yet was somewhat glad of it, since he feared that the Consul might call him to account. Just as he found no pretext for talking things over with the Consul, so he found no words to address to Shoshanah. It was not that she avoided him, but that she showed him no overt sign of good will. Or if she indeed wished him well, she gave him no opportunity for speaking out. How was it that Shoshanah managed to put him off; how was it that he could not bring himself to speak? Only because when they were together their conversation never led up to that principle point; when he parted from her, there he was in just the same position as the day before and the day before that. What should I do? he would think. What should I do? But since no answer was forthcoming, he would leave this for time to decide. It should be said that Rechnitz was not particularly passive, but since he knew the decision was not his alone, he left it for the moment when Shoshanah would play her part.

The Consul and his daughter did not continue with their travels. It was clear that they meant to settle down, and now there was a coming and going of house agents carrying plans of apartments and houses. When Rechnitz saw these people he felt ashamed. He had boasted about the kind of person the Consul would find in the Land of Israel and now he had to admit that there *were* some Jews there who did not belong to the "spiritual center." But the Consul found no fault with them. A man had to live and what else could these poor devils do in a poverty-stricken country? When a bit of profit was coming their way, they would twist their words and tell lies whether they wanted to or not.

Meanwhile the Consul and his daughter stayed on in the hotel. Two or three times a week Rechnitz was invited to join them for a meal, sometimes for lunch, sometimes for dinner. When Shoshanah was not present, her father would say to Jacob, "The child is tired, she has a headache." And his tone was sadder than the words suggested.

One day a strange thing happened. The three of them were seated together talking; Shoshanah suddenly fell silent and dropped off to sleep in the middle of what she was saying. At first Rechnitz thought she had merely closed her eyes, as she sometimes did in the course of conversation. The next day Jacob saw old Dr. Hofmann walking out of the hotel together with Herr Ehrlich. After the doctor had taken his leave, the Consul noticed Rechnitz. "So you're here?" he said, and then, "Sit down Jacob, sit down," and then, "Today we shall take our meal without Shoshanah. She has a headache." Many times before, the Consul had sat down to his meal without his daughter; now he behaved as if this were something new, and as distressing as it was new.

Over their meal, the Consul made a special effort to entertain his guest, as if Shoshanah's absence imposed upon him a double duty of hospitality. When they had finished, he drew Jacob over to the sofa at the end of the lounge and talked to him about the United States and New York and the chair which awaited him there, as well as about Kaiser Wilhelm's project for teacher-exchanges between universities.

"I have never asked you," said the Consul, "what led you to your special field of interest?"

Jacob answered, "I was doing botanical studies and from botany I came to work on water plants; that's to say, I turned from higher to lower species of plants, and so to marine vegetation." As he spoke Jacob forgot that there had been another reason besides this.

"And do these plants," said the Consul, "also have their characteristic diseases?"

Rechnitz replied, "There isn't a single thing in creation that is not liable to disease."

Suddenly Jacob's eyes grew round with wonder. A new perspective opened up beyond the one he saw before him, like the vision of a painter struggling to apprehend what his eyes have never seen. The pond in the Consul's garden, whose water plants used to fascinate and amaze him, came back into his memory. Perhaps, after all, his heart had been drawn to these plants since those very days? Twenty years and more had passed since he had first gone down with Shoshanah to the pond and drawn up the wet vegetation; the strange thing about it was that in all those years the thought had never come back into his mind. At that moment he saw before his eyes the same circular pond set in the garden among the shrubs and flowers, with Shoshanah picking flowers and braiding garlands; now Shoshanah jumped into the pond and disappeared; and now she rose again, covered with wet seaweed like a mermaid, the water streaming from her hair. As he thought of her hair, he thought, too, of how on that same day Shoshanah had taken a curl from her curls and, with it, a lock of his forelock, and mingled them and burned them together and they had eaten the ashes and sworn to be faithful to each other. Like the ashes of her hair and of his own which Shoshanah had intermingled, so the day of their vow was blended with the day by the sea when she had reminded him of it. As Jacob sat reflecting, the Consul took out his watch and said, "You look tired. No need to be ashamed of it. A young man like you needs plenty of sleep."

When Jacob got up to leave, the Consul said, "I can see that I shall not be staying here long. Perhaps we shall soon be leaving for Vienna. But as long as we are here we shall be happy to have your company any time at all."

Jacob asked in a low voice, "How is Shoshanah's health?"

The Consul looked at him hard and answered, "If I only knew!" And again he looked at him as if he knew more than he would say.

XXV

What Shoshanah's father did not tell him, others did. A grave affliction had overtaken her, a sickness which had not been heard of before in the Land of Israel. Her head was dizzy and she had lost full control of her legs, which tottered as she moved about. When she spoke, her voice was indistinct and sounded like someone talking in his sleep; indeed, her only desire was for sleep. She would doze off at any time, on any occasion, in the midst of conversation, while walking or while taking a meal. Sometimes she would sleep for days on end, and after waking up would fall asleep again. Zablodovsky the doctor, Raya's father, said, "This disease seems so suspicious to me that I hesitate to call it by its name. The Ehrlich girl has come from a geographical region which leads me to fear that we have here a case of sleeping sickness. I could bring evidence to support what I say by means of a blood test, but from the symptoms themselves I should say that she has been bitten by a poisonous insect. The patient, I hear, sleeps a great deal, even for days on end; she eats and drinks after awakening, and there is a marked change in her disposition, for she was always full of life and is now apathetic. Perhaps you will say, 'But her appearance has not changed and she is no less beautiful than before.' But when I was a medical student didn't I see sufferers from this disease in its early stages who kept their normal appearance for several months without change? If we waste no time in treating the disease at its outset, we can still control it and cure her. There are certain mineral salts, derived from precious metals, which we can inject into the body until the poison is exhausted and the patient's health restored."

Shoshanah's sickness caused no public alarm and her nursing gave rise to no difficulty, but she was in need of careful supervision. She was put to bed in her room with a nurse to watch over her, and everyone who passed by the room moved very softly, so as not to disturb the invalid and so as to catch something of her slumbering presence.

As for Rechnitz, he pays his calls on Shoshanah's father, as he did years ago, except that then he would visit him twice yearly and now he comes twice a week. The Consul treats him even more cordially now and talks away on any topic that his mind prompts into words, or that words call up in his mind. So he describes his travels and the various kinds of people he has encountered. What extraordinary things he has seen. Even at the doorstep of his house, a man may behold such things as sometimes lead him to doubt his own eyes; how much more so when he travels into strange and far-off lands. At times the Consul repeats the same story, or confuses persons and places; for having known and seen so much, he is liable to substitute one person for another or this place for that. And when he says, "Now I am going to tell you something I have never talked about before," you may be sure that he will go over the same story he has related a hundred and one times already. Or he will stop in mid-course, look up alertly, and say, "Haven't I already told you this? It's hard on me, Rechnitz, the way you let me run on about things you've already heard." Then Jacob will answer, "Not at all, it's quite new to me." So the Consul returns to his story without misgivings. But even if he remembers having told it before, he continues just the same. It is like those songs we sing all our lives; they stir our spirits and remind us of the time we sang them first. The hotel servants come up and remove the loaded ash tray in front of him, replacing it with an empty one. In a deferential whisper they ask, "Would the Consul care for anything?" and withdraw as silently as they came.

Sometimes the Consul would call back the old days when Frau Ehrlich was still alive. When he spoke of those times his description was accurate in every detail, there were no slips; the miracle happened and the past was present once again. Jacob asked no questions about Shoshanah and her father made no mention of her. But now and then he would clutch his head and say, "Any pain's better than a pain in the head," as if he had become a partner in Shoshanah's suffering.

Once before Purim, Rechnitz was about to leave for one of those field trips in which teachers and their students take part together at this time of year. There is no better time for them; mountains and valleys, hills and groves are covered with green and all the country blossoms like God's own garden. Before going away, Rechnitz came to say goodbye. The Consul gazed at him with admiration. "You look as fresh and blooming as a young god," he exclaimed. He took Jacob by the arm and led him out into the garden. The young man seemed to him a personification of spring, when the entire world is made new. He, too, would gladly renew himself; if not in the mountains and the valleys, at least in the garden of his hotel.

The flowers were all in blossom, the lemon trees gave off their scent, the spikes of the palm trees reached up to the blue sky, and the sky itself seemed to blossom over every tree and bush. So deeply moved was the Consul that he could hardly find words to speak, beyond exclaiming at the beauty of this tree or that bush. Suddenly he reached out his hand in a gesture of helplessness, saying, "And there Shoshanah lies, unable to see all the things that we can." A sigh broke from Jacob as he asked, "How is Shoshanah now?"

The Consul took Jacob's hand in his. "Never," he said, "have I wished for a better husband for my daughter. But…"

Jacob lowered his eyes and waited. There was a pause, the pause continued, and still Shoshanah's father did not speak. Jacob raised his head again and looked up. Shoshanah's father became aware of him and said with a sigh, "Soon we are going to Vienna to see Nothnagel. Let's pray that he can find a cure for her disease. And you, my son," he went on, "here you are…" But the words failed him. He remembered a letter that Jacob's parents had written to him and tried to recall its contents, but could not bring them to mind. To Jacob he said, "Let me put it to you in this way. Suppose I am holding on to some valuable object, which I am about to return to its rightful owner. Suddenly the object slips from my hands before it has reached the owner and there we are, both left empty-handed; I who had it in my grasp and he who reached out to take it." While he spoke he looked down at his hands as if puzzling over how they had let it slip. Finally he extended his right hand to Rechnitz by way of farewell, and said, "Let's go now." Yet he held on to Rechnitz's hand, as old people do, clinging to the warmth that has come their way. And Rechnitz perceived this and was glad that he had this warmth to offer.

The Consul for his part became aware that Rechnitz still stood expectant. He saw in Rechnitz a healthy, fresh-cheeked young man in all his vigor, at a time when Shoshanah was perhaps more seriously ill than the doctor would admit. His expression changed suddenly to resentment. What does he want of me? he thought. He let his hand fall and said briefly, "Goodbye."

Rechnitz parted from the old man feeling dejected, for never before had he been treated in this way. As he was going he heard the Consul call after him. Conflicting thoughts entered his mind; hope and expectation, and against this, anxiety and grief, which told him that if he turned back he would hear what was better left unheard. "Oh God," he prayed under his breath, "save me in your great mercy."

The Consul said, "I meant to tell you that when you are back from your walking tour you must not forget to come to us."

Rechnitz laid a hand to his heart and replied, "I shall come."

The Consul shook hands with him again, wished him a successful trip and showed by his expression that all his former affection had returned. Rechnitz, too, was calm again. Now, he thought, I must set about making the arrangements for my journey. He began reckoning up all the articles he must take with him. At first they came to mind in a confused jumble, but in the end they sorted themselves out of their own accord and there was no need to make a second reckoning.

XXVI

No change, no alteration in Shoshanah's condition. She would sleep for days on end, or if she awoke, it was only to fall asleep again.

Good God, what harm had Shoshanah done that You punish her so? If it was for her haughty bearing, wasn't this an effect of the disease itself, which makes it harder to behave with normal friendliness towards others? Who would suppose that this charming girl, whose lids close over eyes so beautiful that no man seems worthy to behold them, whose figure has the stateliness of a solitary palm tree, is fated to sleep out her days?

Thus Shoshanah lies in her bed and everyone who passes her room walks softly. Many days have gone by since Jacob last saw her; meanwhile her father has aged beyond his years. Although he has not been visited with the sickness of his daughter, he has lost his capacity for staying awake. When most men are fully alert, he is liable to drop off to sleep, even in the middle of speaking. Bestirring himself, he will sigh and say, "At night when I want to sleep I lie awake, and in the daytime when I want to talk to people I can't resist the desire for sleep."

Rechnitz saw his embarrassment and began to keep away from the hotel. Yet when he called to inquire about him, the Consul refrained from asking why he had not been round in the last day or two. There was no change in their relationship; in fact, the Consul felt a new kind of affection for Jacob, but the old age which had so suddenly fallen upon him inevitably left its mark.

When the university appointment was first made public, everybody showed even more friendliness towards Jacob than before, and this without any designs for themselves or their daughters. They recognized that Dr. Rechnitz was intended for Shoshanah Ehrlich and there was nothing to be done about it. But when Shoshanah fell sick, they again began to regard him in the old light. Sometimes the expectations of parents have a solid basis, sometimes not, and new hopes grow out of their very despair. The sleep into which Shoshanah Ehrlich had fallen served to awaken such parental hopes. For their daughters, however, it was different. Of all their expectations nothing remained in their hearts but a sense of loss as they looked ahead to Rechnitz's departure.

Rechnitz now made his arrangements for the journey to America. On the way, he planned a stopover in Europe to visit his father and mother. Three years had gone by since he had seen them, for any holiday trips he had made were to the marine biology station in Naples, and not to his home. From the day he first hinted to his mother that he might be arriving, she had taken to sitting at her window reading his letters, one after another, or rereading the letter which the Consul had sent her from Jaffa. At this same time, Jacob in Jaffa was picturing himself as a child again with Shoshanah. In her short frock, she chased butterflies, picked flowers and made a crown of them for her head. Actually, the Consul's house now stood desolate and empty and Rechnitz's parents had long since moved out of that neighborhood. But whenever his father's home came to his mind, he saw it still as standing next to the Consul's.

Meanwhile, Rechnitz turned back to his work. He was busy at his microscope, and happy, for sometimes small things give us great happiness, especially when they link together into something large. The humble sea plants with their tints of green, red, brown and blue, which have neither taste nor scent, and are without any counterpart on land, were dearer to Rechnitz than all the trees, bushes and shrubs of the earth. Out of the strength of his love, and his capacity to take unqualified delight in the smallest of things, his own soul grew and perfected itself ever more. And with this wholeness of spirit came tranquility. Once again he surveyed, examined and tested, with an undistracted love, objects which he had set aside for many days, perhaps since the day when Shoshanah Ehrlich came to Jaffa. Science is a complacent mistress who is not jealous of others; when you return to her you find what is not to be found in a thousand rivals. How many days and weeks had these sea plants lain, floating in salt water within their oblong trays of clear glass, exuding their salt water like tears! But now that Rechnitz had returned and wiped their tears away, they looked up at him so lovingly that in their presence he forgot any other concern.

Jaffa, darling of the waters, is crowded with men of all communities, busy at trade and labor, at shipping and forwarding, each pursuing his own ends, absorbed in his own task. There are others who take no part in any of these activities: such is Jacob Rechnitz. Yet even he is not idle; you might even say that he is busier than all the rest. What need is there for those plants he is so concerned with?

The stars adorn the sky and provide light for the world and those who dwell in it, the flowers adorn the earth and give off their good scent; for this the stars and the flowers were created. But those weeds of the sea, which have neither scent nor taste, what good is to be found in them? Yet far away from Jaffa, from the Land of Israel, there are men who make a study of seaweed, just as Rechnitz does, men who value his activities and pay him honor and esteem.

XXVII

In honor of Rechnitz, all his colleagues, as well as the school trustees, got together and arranged a farewell party. At first they meant to hold it in the Hotel Semiramis, but finally they settled on the schoolhouse where Rechnitz had taught.

They seated Rechnitz at the head of the table with the two principals to his left and right and all the other teachers and trustees in order of precedence. The table was spread with an array of wines and cakes, oranges, almonds, pistachio nuts and various fruits of the season.

The first principal rose to his feet and said, "Gentlemen, we all know the reason why we are assembled here. One of our number, who has spent the last three years with us, is now leaving us. There is no need for me to say how much we regret this, but our joy is equal to our regret for we know that he is going to a great and honored position. We too gain credit from his advance, so I raise my glass and drink a toast to him, to us all, and to our school – a school where we have such teachers as Rechnitz!"

After the toast had been drunk, the second principal began as follows: "My colleague has said that our joy is as great as our regret, since our friend here has been advanced to a great and honored position, namely, to a certain university abroad. But for my part, I admit to feeling sad. Why is Rechnitz departing? Because we have no university here. If there were one, he would not have to leave us; he would join our own university and teach there. My dear colleagues, I am raising an issue which, after all, needs to be frankly discussed. Why have we no university? Because we are content with too little and therefore get nothing at all. I know that people make fun of me for wanting a university. Why do they laugh? Is there any enterprise of ours which they don't deride? When we founded our school here, did they not laugh at us? Did they not call us charlatans? Now those who mocked us come begging for posts. I am not saying, of course, that a university is the same as a high school. No two things in the world are completely alike – except for the smart-alecks and scoffers, who are the same in all places and times. Today they laugh, tomorrow they are dumb-founded, the day after tomorrow they see what they can get out of it for themselves. Finally, they boast that it was they who suggested the whole idea. Let me say in conclusion that I hope we, too, will achieve a university before long to which we can invite our friend Rechnitz to come and lecture. What a great university that will be, when all the scholars of Israel, from all the universities of the world, gather in Jerusalem, on the Temple Mount, to teach wisdom and knowledge! Such a university, my dear friends, the eye has not beheld. But it follows of necessity that I mean no mere seminary for religious studies. We have enough already of this 'religious study' stuffed into us morning, noon and night. When I say university, I mean a real one, where all the forms of knowledge to be found in other centers of learning will be taught. And at this point let me turn to our colleague Rechnitz. My dear Rechnitz, just as we regret that you are leaving us, so shall we rejoice on the day you return here to our own university. 'Blessed be your going out and your coming in.' To your health!"

After this speech the hall rang with cheers. At last there was silence again, the toast was drunk, and speech followed speech until, when midnight had passed, the company went home quietly.

XXVIII

Ever since the Consul's coming to Jaffa, Rechnitz had given up visiting the homes he used to frequent. He had started by being available to the Consul at all hours; now he neglected him, too, and stayed in his room devoting himself entirely to his work. He would take up some piece of seaweed, cut it and examine it under the microscope, then attach it to a sheet of paper, fold the sheet, place it in his great album and note down its name, its habitat, and the date when he had drawn it out of the sea. Nearly two hundred separate species had been taken by Rechnitz from the sea near Jaffa, Haifa, Acre, Caesarea, Hadera and elsewhere. It would hardly be an exaggeration to say that no one in the entire world possessed as many sea plants of the Mediterranean as Jacob Rechnitz. Nowadays we are familiar with more than two hundred kinds of Mediterranean seaweed, and the specialists know of still more. But in his time, no one had a collection to match that of Rechnitz. There they were, dried, attached to their sheets, placed in the album. At first glance you would think you were looking into an artist's sketch book, each line was drawn with such exquisite care and beauty; for the way of seaweeds is to adhere to paper, become absorbed in it, and not protrude from the surface. But once you drop a little water on them, they grow soft and you see before you living plants, the work of the Creator who cares as much for each humble object as He does for what is high and mighty. There were times when Rechnitz shed a tear in his rapture, which fell on the plant and brought it to life again.

The sea gave forth its daily harvest, and at night, under the moon, the daughters of Jaffa took their walks by the shore. The waves kissed their footprints and tossed up an abundance of plants such as Rechnitz had been used to gather. But you will not find Rechnitz there; he is well content with what he has taken to his room and laid out upon his table. Happy, at ease among his glass trays of saltwater, he sits with the great album before him, its pages full. That album is the bliss of his eye and soul.

This was all that Rechnitz did; he sat in his room and devoted himself to his work. At times he was so preoccupied that he would forget to light the little burner to make his coffee or, if he lit it, to put coffee in the pot before the water boiled over and put out the flame. Needless to say, he no longer took tea with the parents of his pupils and girl friends; thus, he made himself a stranger in all those households and with all those good people who, though they seemed unimportant then, were to count for much in the days to come. For they dwelt in the Land of Israel and were among the first of its founders. The reasons for their coming were many and varied, but it may well be that the very people whose motives were most obscure will be remembered and inscribed for all time, while those who came specifically for their country's sake will be forgotten and ignored.

Rechnitz turned his thoughts away from these people, and from their daughters too. This time was perhaps the best he ever knew. In his great desire for Shoshanah he had put out of mind all lesser desires; now even that desire fell away. He knew that he must prepare for his journey, whether it be to America or to Europe, for now the Consul was about to leave and it was better to travel with him and Shoshanah than to go alone. And yet work took his mind away from the journeys that lay ahead. People in Jaffa knew that he must get his lectures ready and took care not to disturb him. And Rechnitz too did not trouble himself with fancied needs. If he had found the time for it, he would have given praise and thanks to the gods for dealing with him so well.

XXIX

One night Rechnitz was alone in his room. The doors were closed and the blinds drawn, and the lamp lit up the table and the plants of the sea laid out upon it. This room had once been full of flowers and their scents; now he had in front of him only these odorless plants, together with the material for his course of lectures in America, which he was preparing in advance. This night, apparently so ordinary, was for Rechnitz singled out from all others, for in it he was experiencing what a man knows but once or twice in a lifetime. Having yielded his will to a single desire, the desire itself at last quits him and he is left free from any and all concerns. Never in his life had Rechnitz been so free a man as now; he had separated himself from Rachel and Leah, from Asnat, Raya and the rest, on account of Shoshanah Ehrlich; he had come to despair of Shoshanah because of her disease; his journey lay before him, and yet even this was put out of his thoughts in order that work might be his sole object and end.

We have intimated that Rechnitz was a modest young man and no woman-hunter; still, man is a social being and he may feel more affection for a group of charming girls than for the rest of the world. Sometimes his hidden thoughts may drive him beyond all reason; were he to consider them dispassionately he would be appalled. With the

Consul's arrival reason resumed its proper place for Rechnitz, but at the cost of his tranquility, which was only restored when he returned to his work. Were one to ask how it was possible for Rechnitz not to grieve at Shoshanah's distress, the answer would be this: many factors for which language, however precise, has no name were operating to silence such thoughts.

So Rechnitz sat in his room, at peace with himself and free from all distraction, for he had come to accept the fact of Shoshanah's sickness and distress. The good gods had favored Rechnitz, granting him peace and calm, together with joy in his work. But these favors were not to last long. The gods are envious, and when they see us prosper too much, they send their agents to change our lives. Every man learns this for himself; let those who have not yet done so now witness the case of Rechnitz. Enough, then, of the beauty of this night and the benefits of a tranquil mind; let us tell instead how Rechnitz lost his tranquility.

As Rechnitz sat alone, he heard the sound of a light tap at the door; after the tap, the door opened and Tamara entered. Entered and stood still. Never before had she called upon Rechnitz; never, perhaps, had she been inside a young man's lodgings. One could tell this from her whole stance and from the dim glow that hung like a mist over her features.

Tamara paused on the threshold, waiting to be asked in. Her lips trembled like petals touched with morning dew. Rechnitz did not take her into his arms but he took her by the hands and seated her on the couch. Tamara was a girl of some humility. Never had she dared to think that people took notice of her, certainly not a great scholar like Dr. Rechnitz. No, the only reason for her coming was that she was planning to go abroad, and since he was also leaving, she had gathered up courage and come to visit him.

Tamara had been graduated from the Jaffa high school and was preparing to go to Europe, where she intended to study medicine, an interest she had inherited from her father the doctor. Meanwhile, she had taken up sculpture and clay modeling and now she was finding it hard to decide where her true inclination lay. The body contained so many secrets and her fingers were itching to create shapes; sometimes she dreamed of figures of flesh and blood, sometimes of figures in stone. Rechnitz found Tamara's conversation exciting, even though it contained no exceptional wisdom. He felt a sudden longing to grasp in his arms this body which was so uncertain about what it wanted, and to kiss Tamara full on the lips. It is quite possible that he would have done so, had he not heard footsteps coming up the stairs.

Again there was a sound at the door; this door, which had not opened to visitors for many days and nights, tonight opened twice.

XXX

Rechnitz pulled himself together and behaved as if there were no little Tamara seated in his room. Rachel and Leah came in. They had not intended to pay a call until, passing the house, they heard the sound of conversation and assumed that Rechnitz was not too busy with his work. In this they were certainly correct.

Tamara sat on the edge of the couch. She looked up at Rachel and Leah without animosity or envy; or if there were a trace of envy, it was only what a young girl would feel towards those older than herself who could talk to Jacob without being overawed. Now she lowered her head to sniff at the carnation on her blouse, pleased enough to take her place with Rachel and Leah, her seniors.

Rechnitz moved his basins and seaweed out of the way and transferred his microscope elsewhere. Only a few dry specimens remained on the table, which he did not need, as there were duplicates already mounted in his album. Now that his work was set aside and he had only his guests to attend to, he would gladly have offered them something, as was his usual way, but he could find nothing: no chocolate, no fruit – in fact, since the Consul's arrival he had felt no need for such things. But Zeus, who watches over guests, now intimated to the host that tea might be prepared, for tea is welcome on all occasions. So Rechnitz took out his little burner and set it going. The flame lit up as it used to in the old days when Rachel Heilperin would drop in. Now Rachel sat and gazed, sometimes at the flame which flickered and mounted through the perforations, sometimes at its reflection in the looking-glass opposite, thinking to herself, Rechnitz is going to America and I shall not see him again. Probably he will put me out of his mind and not think of me anymore, just as he never thought of me before he knew me. And probably this is the last time I shall ever sit in this room. She looked up towards Rechnitz but saw only his back, since he was occupied with getting out the tea and sugar. Pursing her lips, which had a way of pouting disdainfully, she picked up two or three of the seaweeds that Rechnitz had left on the table because he could not bring himself to throw them away. Holding them in her hands, she began to plait them together. At the same moment, or even a moment before, Leah Luria got up and took over the entire operation of tea-making, just as she always took every task upon herself.

The little burner stands between the door and the table; the water bubbles and rises, but when it reaches full boil there isn't enough for all the girls, as the kettle is too small. Let us leave the tea, then, and turn to other concerns. There is the burner with the water gradually heating. Opposite, Tamara sits on the edge of the couch. Rachel is at the table, plaiting herself a kind of garland. A song comes into her mind —

> *Beside the brook the boy reclined,*
> *And wove his flowery wreath.*

Then again she wonders at herself for bothering with such plants, whose smell is like that of iodine on a wound.

Leah said, "Here am I standing about as if I had nothing to do and I promised to go and see Asnat!"

Rachel answered, "You are nothing but a parcel of promises, Leah," and went on plaiting her garland.

"But since I promised her, what shall I do? How can I let her wait for nothing?"

"Oh, let Asnat wait until she's tired of waiting. Where are *you* off to, Tamara?"

Tamara answered, "I am going to call Miss Mag-argot. That is, if Dr. Rechnitz has no objections."

"On the contrary," said Rechnitz.

Rachel laughed and said, "I knew that Leah and I would not be enough for you! Whom else shall we invite?"

But just as Tamara was about to leave, in came Asnat, and with her, her relative Raya. For Asnat, deciding not to wait any more, had gone for a walk with Raya Zablodovsky and while they were out they had passed by Rechnitz's house, heard the sound of conversation and decided to come in.

Asnat had not really intended to visit Rechnitz but she was glad now that she had come. And the same was true of Raya, who was not paying a visit for the sake of Rechnitz but to please herself; it was her own personality that guided her movements and so she made herself at home everywhere. Thus it came about that five girls were all met in the lodgings of Rechnitz, each for a reason of her own and all well pleased to be there.

"Is anyone still missing?" asked Rachel.

"If Mira were here," said Leah, "that would make a full session."

"Yes, but there wouldn't be a spare cup for her," said Rachel.

"I don't take tea," Tamara put in.

"My dear child," said Rachel, "yours is not the only mouth."

Tamara lowered her head and took another sniff at the carnation on her blouse.

"I didn't mean to mock you," Rachel added.

Tamara said, "I know that, Miss Heilperin, and of course I'm not hurt."

After tea, Asnat said, "How about going for a walk? All in favor, raise their hands."

"Better their feet," said Rachel, "so that we can get started."

"Let me first make our host's bed," said Leah, "so that when he comes back he'll find it ready for him. Where shall we go?"

"Where?" said Asnat. "By the sea, of course."

"And when we pass Mira's house," added another of the girls, "we'll call her out too. Who votes for that?"

So Rechnitz found himself again in the company of the six. Not long ago he had been glad that he had given them up, now he was pleased that they had returned. The envy of the gods works in devious ways, so that we ourselves cannot know what is for our good and what is not.

XXXI

The sea lay stretched on a bed as wide as the world, its nightshirt the moon-whitened waves. The shores had grown long, moonlight lay on the sands and the sea. A beneficent spirit brooded over Rechnitz and the six maidens, for on the way they had called for Mira, who hurried to make up the quorum of the Seven Planets. When such a night as this and such a spirit are in conjunction, their power is complete, their blessing great.

Rachel, Leah and Asnat walked to the right of Rechnitz; Raya, Mira and Tamara to his left. Sometimes they changed places, those on the left wheeling over to the right, or those on the right passing over to the left, but they always took care to leave Rechnitz in the middle. And Rechnitz among his maidens was carried beyond himself, as he had been on those fine nights a year ago, and two years, and three years ago. At that moment, he put Shoshanah entirely from his mind. But her memory formed a circle around his heart, like the golden lashes around her eyes as she slept.

Rachel Heilperin wore the appearance of being happy, while Leah Luria was happy indeed. "On a night like this…" she cried excitedly, and great untellable longings trembled in that lovely voice. Since she knew no way to sing the praises of the night, she stretched out her delicate arms and stared into the hollow of the universe. And night assigned that hollow its own starlit mightiness. "On a night like this…" she cried again, and again stopped short. But since she could not still the tumult within her, she called to the others, "Girls, girls, just look! Look!"

Sea and sky, heaven and earth, and all the space between were grown into a single living being; a luminous calm enveloped by azure, or an azure transparent as air. Up above, and under the surface of the sea, the moon raced like a frenzied girl. Even the sands were moon-struck and seemed to move perpetually. Like the sands, like all the surrounding air, the girls, and with them Rechnitz, were taken up into the dream. If they looked overhead, there was the moon running her race, and if they looked out to sea, there she was again hovering upon the face of the waters. Heaven and earth, land and sea, had become a single whole; and this was contained in yet another, greater whole that no eye could see.

Rachel took Leah's hand, Leah the hand of Asnat and Asnat that of Raya, and Raya took Mira's, and Mira Tamara's and Tamara took Rachel's; they encircled Rechnitz and danced around him, danced until Rachel broke from their ring and knelt down facing the sea with her eyes uplifted to the moon. Asnat stood still, stretched out her hands in the air and played inaudible notes on an unseen keyboard. "Listen, Tamara," said Mira, "if I had a horse, I would go galloping from one end of the world to the other!"

"Good people all," said Raya, "has anybody a horse in her pocket for Mira? Oh Mira, Mira, I've no horse in my pocket either, so what can I do for you, my dear? Could you possibly do without the horse and go on foot?"

"For your sake, Raya, I shall go on foot," Mira answered, laughing and putting her arms around Tamara. Tamara laid her head on Mira's breast and said, "You're a good friend." "Wait, little one, wait," Raya called to Tamara, "my shoe's full of sand." She leaned against her, took off her shoe and shook it empty.

Suddenly Leah called, "Look, good people all, just look! What's that out to sea? I swear there's a light burning on the water!"

They looked out to sea and at the light, which came from a passing ship. Only those aboard knew whether it was sailing to or from the Land of Israel, but to Jacob Rechnitz and his companions it made no difference where the ship was headed. They stood in silence watching the light floating on the surface of the sea. The spread of waters girdled both the ship and the light. Now the light sank, now it rose, again it sank and floated. On such a ship Jacob would soon be sailing over endless distances, and they, perhaps, would stand on the shore as now and see the light far off, while Jacob would not see them or be aware of their presence, even as the passengers on this ship were unaware of being observed. So the girls stood silent, looking out and clasping each other by the waist. At last they turned their thoughts from the ship and grieved for themselves, as if they had suffered some loss.

Once thoughts have entered the mind, words come to the lips, and Leah spoke aloud what they were all thinking. "I've been wanting to ask you, Dr. Rechnitz," she said, "when will you be leaving for America?"

Rachel said, "How could our doctor make such a long journey just as he is?"

"What do you mean by 'just as he is'?"

"I mean, all alone," said Rachel.

"And what does 'all alone' mean?"

"It means without a wife," said Rachel.

Leah took Jacob's hand and clasped it as a conciliatory gesture.

Rachel added, "What a pity it is we didn't settle among ourselves that whoever first took Rechnitz's hand won the privilege of going to America with him."

Leah withdrew her hand, remarking, "You're a wicked girl, Rachel!"

Asnat said, "But, Leah, doesn't taking his hand make you a wicked girl?"

Then Tamara came up and took hold of Jacob's hand.

"It will do you no good, Tamara," said Rachel. "We were talking about whoever *first* took his hand, which does not apply to you."

Tamara gave the hand a little squeeze and sniffed at the carnation on her blouse.

"I don't know why," said Mira, "but I feel as if I want to run. To run from one end of the world to the other."

"To run? What put that into your head?"

Mira said, "If I were to run, no horse and no rider would ever catch me." Even as she spoke, she started off on her light feet. Leah called after her, "Mira, Mira, don't go too far!" But Mira did not hear her; she was already some distance away and still running.

Said Raya to Tamara, "And you, my little Tamara, stand about like a hobbled bird. Don't you want to try your legs?"

Tamara raised her eyes and gazed up at Jacob to see if her running would please him. Even as she looked, her feet lifted themselves of their own accord and she was off.

Asnat played with the tassels of her belt, swinging them back and forth as she said, "If Dr. Rechnitz doesn't take one of these mighty runners for a wife, I don't know whom he will take." As she spoke, the tassels slipped out of her hands and her legs began to quiver.

"Do you want to run, too?" said Rachel, taunting her.

"If you run, I will!" she answered.

"No," said Rachel, "you run. What's this I am holding, a circle of thorns? Dr. Rechnitz, I forgot I had your plants in my hand and I've brought them out with me. Now listen to me, girls, listen. Whoever beats the others in the race will be crowned with this garland." She raised overhead the seaweeds she had plaited, repeating, "Whoever beats the rest takes this as her crown. What do you want to say, Leah?"

"That's not how the Greeks did it," said Leah. "What they did was this. The young men ran and whoever won the race received the crown from the most beautiful girl present. Isn't that so, Dr. Rechnitz?" And as she spoke she, too, felt her knees quiver. To Rachel she said, "Will you run with me?"

"Run, Leah, run!" said Rachel. "Perhaps you'll win the garland."

At this point the other girls returned. "Girls," said Leah, "if you'd been here a moment ago, you'd have heard a splendid thing."

"And what is this splendid thing we've missed?" asked Asnat.

"Do you see this garland?" said Leah. "We've all agreed that the fastest runner will win and wear this wreath, made of Dr. Rechnitz's weeds. Do you agree, Dr. Rechnitz?"

Rechnitz nodded, saying, "Yes." But his face grew pale and his heart began to quake.

Leah insisted, "The Greeks had the men run, not the girls."

Asnat answered, "But since all those young men are dead and we are alive, let's do their running ourselves. Do you agree, Dr. Rechnitz? Yes or no? Why don't you speak?"

Rechnitz answered, "I agree," and his heart quaked all the more.

"Very well," said Asnat. "Stand in a line, girls. Now, where do we start from and where do we run to?"

She looked up in the direction of the Hotel Semiramis and said, "Let's start from the Semiramis."

"And where do we finish?"

"At the old Moslem cemetery. Dr. Rechnitz, you stand in line with us and call 'one, two, three.' At 'three,' we'll start. Raya, don't step out of line. Tamara, until Rechnitz gives the call you mustn't lift a foot, do you hear?"

"I hear," said Tamara.

"Stay in your place, then, and don't stretch your neck out like a camel's."

All the girls now stood together where the balconies of the Hotel Semiramis overlooked the sea. They faced the old cemetery, which they had taken as their finishing point. Each looked down at her feet as they made room for Rechnitz. And Rechnitz, standing in the middle, looked from side to side at the girls poised for the race, at the garland on Rachel's arm, and again at the girls, wondering which of them would wear it as her crown. His hands trembled and his heart beat so fast that he could hardly speak.

The sand was damp and firmly packed; the moon lay on the dim beach, and the dim beach was its mirror. Like drawn bows to which the arrows had not yet been fitted stood the six girls, each waiting for the word that would set her off. But the word was still unspoken; it seemed that Rechnitz had forgotten all about their agreement of a moment ago, or perhaps he had not forgotten and that was the cause of his delay. One girl asked, "Why is he taking so long?" And another said, "Come on, Dr. Rechnitz, say the word!"

Then Jacob, in fear and trembling, called, "One!" To left and right of him the girls quivered with excitement, so that the very sands beneath their feet quivered too. As for Rechnitz, he too was trembling, and perhaps more than they. Suddenly Rachel cried, "Wait, Jacob, wait!" She left her place, knelt down in front of Rechnitz, took the wreath from her arm and passed it to him before going back to stand with her comrades. "Now, Doctor," she said, "you can say, 'two, three.' " Rechnitz heard her but did not heed, or heeded her but did not hear. Then abruptly the words broke from his lips of their own accord and a voice was heard saying, "One, two, three!" and the girls shot off on their run.

XXXII

Jacob held the garland that Rachel Heilperin had plaited from the dried seaweeds she had found on his table. He looked about him, uncertainly. The six girls raced side by side until one went twisting ahead, like a ball of twine that has dropped from the hands of the knitter. Then she was caught up and returned to the cluster of her companions. Again the rank was broken, by one here and one there, until one girl outpaced all the rest for a time, only to be overtaken; and again the group came together and again broke up. His eyes began to burn painfully; still he watched the running girls. He pricked up his ears to hear the sound of their feet, though this was difficult to catch, for now the tide was rising and the noise of the waves kept breaking through.

At the sound of the waves, at the sight of the limitless expanse of sea, Rechnitz closed his eyes. And now he saw his mother kneeling down before him. He was a small boy; she was threading a new tie round his collar, for it was the day Shoshanah was born and he was invited to the Consul's house. But surely, thought Jacob to himself, she can't be my mother, and it goes without saying that she isn't Shoshanah's mother either, because one is far from here and the other is dead; if I open my eyes I shall see that this is nothing but an optical illusion. The illusion went so far as to present him at once with his own mother and with Shoshanah's; and since one object could not be two, it followed of necessity that here was neither his own mother nor Shoshanah's. But if so, who was she? Shoshanah herself, perhaps? Of course not, for Shoshanah was ill in bed.

He opened his eyes and saw that all was but the shadow of an image, what a man compares to what he actually sees. Of course this was neither his mother nor Shoshanah's mother nor Shoshanah, but Leah and Rachel and Asnat and Raya and Mira and Tamara. Jacob shifted the wreath from one hand to the other and looked across at the girls who were racing side by side, or one close after the other, each trying to outstrip her companion. Rachel was as light-footed as a gazelle; it seemed likely that she would outrun the rest. But Leah, the deliberate one who measured all her movements, now passed Rachel, and Mira overtook Leah, naturally enough, since she was so accustomed to exercise and running. Finally she was left behind Asnat, with Rachel and Raya outstripping them both. Little Tamara vanished into thin air, she was swallowed up in space; but again she appeared, only to be swallowed up again and vanish from sight. Yet apparently she had managed to pass her companions. At first it had made no difference to Jacob who would outrun whom; now he felt some regret as he saw Tamara beating them all. At least there was some comfort in the thought that the old cemetery was far away and that one of her friends would probably get ahead before she could reach it. Indeed, a figure was now to be seen running ahead of Tamara, but since she was a good way off one could not tell quite who she was. Jacob shut his eyes and left it for time to decide. But time waited and did not defer to Jacob.

A good while passed. Rechnitz stood motionless. What has happened? he wondered. By now they should have returned, but they are not here yet. He looked around him. Heaven and earth, land and sea, were all confounded, and the waves of the sea were raised on high, the waves crashed like thunder, and the sound of the girls' running feet could not be heard. Why haven't they come back? he asked himself. The sea grew even vaster, its waves rubbed against the dry land, but there was no sound of the girls' feet, no sight of the girls themselves. Where had they gone, where had they vanished?

Rechnitz hung the wreath over his arm and began to run. He ran until he reached the place and found them all there, as well as one who had not been with them at the start. She was in her night-gown, like a maiden suddenly alarmed in her sleep. Silent and fearful stood the girls, and with them stood Shoshanah Ehrlich, who had outstripped them all in the race. Neither Leah nor Rachel nor Asnat nor Raya nor Mira nor Tamara had seen her running, yet each of them had been aware in the course of the race that someone was ahead of her, without knowing this someone as Shoshanah Ehrlich, Jacob's friend, who for many days and weeks had been asleep, never rising from her bed. With fear in their souls they forgot the garland and their agreement with Jacob. And Jacob, too, forgot all this as he stood before Shoshanah.

Suddenly there was a voice calling him by name, a voice that came, as it were, from beneath Shoshanah's eyelashes. Jacob shut his eyes and replied in a whisper, "Shoshanah, are you here?"

Shoshanah's eyelashes signaled assent. She put out her hands, took the crown from Jacob's arm and placed it on her head.

Here, for the time being, we have brought to an end our account of the affairs of Jacob Rechnitz and Shoshanah Ehrlich. These are the same Shoshanah and Jacob who were betrothed to one another through a solemn vow. Because of it, we have called this whole account "Betrothed," though at first we had thought to call it "The Seven Maidens."

Annotations to "Betrothed"

3. Jaffa / An ancient port city, and main center of the Second *Aliyah* and Jewish settlement in the early 20th century; today the southernmost part of the modern municipality of Tel Aviv-Jaffa. Agnon lived in Jaffa when he first arrived in the Land of Israel in 1908, roughly the same time as the setting of this story.

3. Daily cover / Cf. Deuteronomy 33:12.

3. Ishmaelites / Muslims.

3. Jacob Rechnitz / As with many of Agnon's characters, it is likely that the author has encoded a form of "midrash" into our protagonist's name. Jacob is reminiscent of the Biblical forefather, whose name (*Ya'akov* in Hebrew) carries a meaning of "to circumvent" or to be "crooked" (Genesis 25:26, but also 27:36). Recall that the Biblical Jacob was manipulated to marry a woman against his will (Genesis 29), as is that other scholar in Agnon's writing, Akavia Mazal – whose first name is etymologically identical with Ya'akov/ Jacob – in "In the Prime of her Life" in *Two Scholars Who Were in Our Town and Other Novellas* (Toby Press, 2014). Rechnitz is a town in Austrian Burgenland, near the Hungarian border, but may evoke *"recht"* meaning right or proper. If so, Jacob Rechnitz's name embodies the coincidence of opposites: a crooked uprightness, and may recall Agnon's early novella of misaligned love, "And the Crooked Shall be Made Straight" (*VeHaya He'Akov LeMishor*, cf. Isaiah 40:4), forthcoming in translation from Toby Press. Avraham Holtz suggests that Rechnitz might be a Hebrew anagram for *nitzrakh* – meaning "needy".

4. Fever of land speculation / Wave of land speculation in and around 1891, coordinated by *Hovevei Zion* leader Ze'ev (Vladimir) Tiomkin (1861–1927), leading to the Ottoman Government forbidding land sales in Palestine to Jews, resulting in widespread bankruptcies.

Ze'ev Tiomkin

4. Turk / The Ottoman Turks ruled the Land of Israel from 1517 to 1917.

4. Council of the Lovers of Zion in Odessa / The *Hovevei Zion* (Lovers of Zion) were European Zionist groups, founded in the 1880s to promote Jewish immigration and agricultural settlement in Palestine. The Odessa Committee was the branch of the movement in Russia, recognized as an official charity by the authorities.

5. *HaShilo'ah* / Monthly Hebrew journal founded by Asher Ginsberg (Ahad Ha'Am) in 1896, covering Jewish life, literature and culture.

HaShilo'ah

5. *Razsvyet* / "The Dawn"; Russian-language Zionist weekly, published in St. Petersburg between 1907–10.

6. My vineyard / Cf. Song of Songs 1:6.

6. Caulerpa / A genus of seaweeds in the family Caulerpaceae, the name means "creeping stem".

6. Cryptogam / A plant that reproduces by spores, without flowers or seeds.

7. Hovered over the face of the waters / Cf. Genesis 1:2.

Caulerpa prolifera

7. Ehrlich / German family name meaning "honest" or "honorable" or "upright"; cf. meaning of Jacob Rechnitz's name, above.

8. Solemn vow / It is from this Hebrew phrase, *shevu'at emunim*, that the story takes its title; the English title "Betrothed" captures this partially in its etymology "to pledge troth", to make a vow or oath of faithfulness.

9. Rose / The symbolism of the rose is lost in translation; in Hebrew a rose is *shoshanah*, the name of our story's female protagonist.

10. Katharinenhof / A resort outside of Vienna.

Franz Joseph I

10. Emperor / Franz Joseph I (1830–1916), Emperor of the Austro-Hungarian Empire.

13. There is a time for all... / Ecclesiastes 3:1.

13. Great War / World War I.

14. Sappho / Greek lyric poetess from the island of Lesbos, c. 630–570 BCE.

14. Medea / In Greek mythology, Medea was the daughter of King Aeëtes of Colchis and granddaughter of the sun god Helios, and later wife to the hero Jason (of Argonaut fame). She is the central character in Euripides's play *Medea*.

14. Yeshivas / Traditional Talmudic academies. (Many of the eastern European Jews who arrived in the Land of Israel during the early 20th century left behind their traditional learning and strict religious lifestyle.)

Ahad Ha'am

14. Seven Planets / Classical heavenly bodies visible to the eye and known in the ancient world: Mercury, Venus, Mars, Jupiter and Saturn, together with the Sun and Moon; cf. Shabbat 156a for Talmudic astrology and mentions of these seven planets.

16. Intimate *du* / Conversations between Rechnitz and the Ehrlichs would have taken place in German, which differentiates between the informal *du* for second-person address and the more formal *Sie*.

Moshe Leib Lilienblum

21. Ahad Ha'Am / Pen-name of Asher Ginsberg (1856–1927), journalist, essayist, and preeminent Zionist thinker; founder of "cultural Zionism" aiming toward the establishment of a "Spiritual Center" as opposed to Herzl's political Zionism. The pen-name Ahad Ha'Am (taken from Genesis 26:10) means "one of the people".

21. Lilienblum / Moshe Leib Lilienblum (1843–1910), writer and figure in the

Jewish Enlightenment movement and leader of the *Hovevei Zion* in Russia.

21. Ussishkin / Menachem Ussishkin (1863–1941), Russian-born Zionist leader and head of the Jewish National Fund which was responsible for land acquisition in Palestine

22. Jerusalem Talmud / Rabbinic commentary on the Mishnah, composed in the 4th–5th centuries in the Land of Israel; counterpart to the later, and more authoritative, Babylonian Talmud.

22. Collector of donations and tithes / Kashrut supervisor who assured that the various agricultural tithes from produce of the Land of Israel were properly separated.

22. Baron Rothschild / Baron Edmond James de Rothschild (1845–1934), French-born member of the Rothschild banking clan, and a strong supporter of Zionism. His charitable support aided the movement and helped establish various settlements and agricultural endeavors in the Land of Israel.

Baron Rothschild

23. Political Zionists / Followers of Theodor Herzl's platform at the First Zionist Congress (Basel, 1897), which aimed at establishing a politically and legally assured Jewish homeland in Palestine.

23. Uganda schism / 1903 proposal to create a Jewish homeland in a portion of British East Africa. The plan created a major schism within the larger Zionist movement, drawing support from Herzl, and opposition from Ussishkin and others. Ultimately rejected at the 1905 Seventh Zionist Congress.

23. Zionists of Zion / Nickname for the followers of Ussishkin; opponents to the Uganda Plan, who remained loyal to the notion that Zionism could only be fulfilled in the Land of Israel.

23. Bilu / Zionist movement to promote agricultural settlement in the Land of Israel, founded by students in 1882 in Kharkov.

24. Galicia / Geographic region comprising parts of contemporary southern Poland and western Ukraine, historical home to a large Jewish population (including Agnon himself).

25. Mikveh or Sarona / Mikveh Israel was the first Jewish agricultural school in Israel, established on the eastern outskirts of Jaffa in 1870. Sarona was a German Templer colony founded in 1871, about 4 km. northeast of Jaffa; today a neighborhood of Tel Aviv.

26. Rays of sunrise / Cf. Yoma 28b and Rashi s.v. "*Timor*".

29. Sefardim / Descendants of the Spanish Jewish community, expelled from Spain in 1492.

29. Ashkenazim / Jews of the central and eastern European tradition.

Jaffa orange logo from Sarona

Yemenite Jew, late 19th c.

29. Yemenite Jews / Members or descendents of the ancient Jewish communities of Yemen (which began emigration to the Land of Israel in 1881). The community follows distinct religious traditions which separate their practices from that of the Ashkenazim and Sefardim. Many Yemenite Jews were known for their skills as craftsmen and artisans, a role they played in the early Settlement.

29. Thou hast set a boundary... / Psalms 104:9 and cf. Rashi.

30. Rishon LeZion / Coastal farm settlement established to the south of Jaffa in 1882; under Baron Rothschild's patronage the Carmel-Mizrahi winery was founded there.

30. Old Baron / Apparently this character is a conflation of two historical figures: Moritz Hall (1838–1914) and his son-in-law Baron Plato von Ustinov (1840–1918), a Russian-born German citizen, and grandfather of the actor Peter Ustinov. Ustinov was the owner of the Hôtel du Parc in Jaffa, renowned for its gardens

Hôtel du Parc

and talking parrots; presumably the setting for "Betrothed". Hall, a Jew from Cracow, was a cannon-caster of King Negus Tewodros II of Ethiopia, where he was converted to Protestantism. He married an Ethiopian court-lady Katharina *née* Zander (1850–1932), who was of mixed Ethiopian-German origin. The character of the Old Baron in Jaffa also appears in Agnon's epic novel of the Second *Aliyah*, *Temol Shilshom* (translated by Barbara Harshav as *Only Yesterday* [Princeton University Press, 2000]). For more on the historical background of these characters see the monograph by Avraham Holtz and Toby Berger Holtz, *Moritz Hall: The Old Man of Jaffa* (University of Haifa, 2003).

Moritz Hall (courtesy T. Holtz)

31. Settlement Bank / Jewish Colonial Trust, which provided loans to Jewish farmers and helped promote construction and settlement, was established in London by the second Zionist Congress in 1899 as the financial instrument of the Zionist Organization. Later incorporated as the present-day Bank Leumi.

34. *Allah kareem* / Arabic: God is the most generous.

34. Japheth / Son of the Biblical Noah (Genesis 5:32); according to folkloric tradition he was the founder and eponym of the ancient city of Jaffa.

35. Nebuchadnezzar / Nebuchadnezzar II (c. 634–562 BCE), king of the Babylonian Empire, responsible for the destruction of the First Temple in Jerusalem, and forced exile of the Jewish tribes (also renowned for the construction of the Hanging Gardens of Babylon).

37. Asclepius / Greek god of medicine and healing; son of Apollo.

40. Ilyushin the taxidermist / Walter Lever, this story's translator, changed this character's name in order to preserve in English an element of the word-play Ilyushin-Illusion (in chapter 22, p. 57) which is generated from Shoshanah's misunderstanding or mispronouncing of his name. In Hebrew the character is named Arzef, and appears in a significant, if minor, role in Agnon's *Temol Shilshom* – see especially Book II Chapter 7.3 (pp. 241–244 in *Only Yesterday*) and Book IV Chapter 15.2 (pp. 604–608) – where he is

portrayed as a craftsman and scientist fully devoted to his work and research by being fully unencumbered by family life:

Arzef lives alone like the First Adam in the Garden of Eden, with no wife and no sons and no cares and no troubles, among all kinds of livestock and animals and birds and insects and reptiles and snakes and scorpions. He dwells with them in peace, and even when he takes their soul, they don't demand his blood in exchange, since they enter the great museums of Europe because of him, and professors and scholars flock to his door and give him honorary degrees and money. Arzef doesn't run after money and doesn't brag about the honorary degrees. Let those who get all their honor from others brag about them. It's enough for Arzef to look at his handiwork and know that never in his life has he ruined any creature in the world, on the contrary, he gave a name and remainder to some birds of the Land of Israel who were said to have vanished from the earth" (*Only Yesterday*, p. 242).

Compare this to the personality of our Dr. Rechnitz and his seaweeds!

It was rumored that Agnon modeled Arzef on Yisrael Aharoni (1882–1946), a Russian-born naturalist, known as the "first Hebrew  zoologist", having discovered and coined Hebrew names for dozens of previously unknown animals, birds, and insects. He emigrated to Jerusalem in 1901, ultimately obtaining an academic post at the Hebrew University. Typically, Agnon neither denied nor confirmed this, see *MeAtzmi el Atzmi* (Schocken, 2000), p. 468.

Yisrael Aharoni

41. *Sanin* / 1907 Russian novel by Mikhail Petrovich Artsybashev (1878–1927); censored for its scandalous erotic and revolutionary content, making it particularly popular with young readers.

43. Otto Weininger and his book *Sex and Character* / Weininger (1880–1903) was a Jewish-born Viennese philosopher. His book *Sex and Character*, published the same year as his suicide,

attempts a scientific argument that all people are composed of both male and the female characteristics. Having converted to Protestantism the year before publication, Weininger analyzes the archetypal Jew as "feminine" – Christianity is described as "the highest expression of the highest faith", while Judaism is called "the extreme of cowardliness". Weininger decries the decay of modern times, and attributes much of it to feminine, or "Jewish", influences.

45. Kirov / City and the administrative center of Kirov Oblast, Russia, located on the Vyatka River, about 950 km. northeast of Moscow.

45. Ibsen / Henrik Ibsen (1828–1906), Norwegian playwright and predominate force in European realism and modernism on the stage and in literature.

46. Sharon settlements / The Sharon region is the northern half of Israel's coastal plain.

48. *Herrchen* / German for "My Lord", but can also mean a pet-owner.

51. Western Wall / Alt. Wailing Wall; remnant of the ancient retaining wall surrounding the Jerusalem Temple, destroyed in 70 CE.

51. Sha'arei Zedek Hospital / Founded on Jaffa Road in 1902, the first major medical facility in Jerusalem outside the walls of the Old City.

Dr. Moshe Wallach (in 1956)

51. A certain doctor / Presumably the founder and long-time director of Sha'arei Zedek, Dr. Moshe (Moritz) Wallach (1866–1957).

56. Ein Rogel / Natural spring and ancient water source on the southeastern outskirts of the Old City of Jerusalem (see Samuel II 17:17, e.g.).

57. Our days on earth are like a shadow / Cf. Chronicles II 29:15.

60. Opened a book… nobody dreams of himself as dead / Presumably Freud's 1899 *The Interpretation of Dreams*, which actually states the opposite of what Shoshanah claims (likely a deliberate "mistake" by Agnon).

63. Nietzsche / Friedrich Nietzsche (1844–1900) was appointed professor of classical philology at the University of Basel at the age of 24, even prior to completing his Ph.D.

Kaiser Wilhelm II

65. Kaiser Wilhem / Wilhem II (1859–1941), last German Emperor and King of Prussia (reigned 1888–1918).

66. Sworn to be faithful / It is from this Hebrew phrase, *shevu'at emunim*, that the story takes its title.

68. Any pain's better than a pain in the head / Shabbat 11a.

68. Nothnagel / Dr. Hermann Nothnagel (1841–1905), German-born internist and professor in Vienna. The family name is German for an "emergency nail" or "nail in need" – an iron spike carried by firefighters of old to be used when an escape from an upper floor was blocked. It could be hammered into an outside window so that a rope could be lowered from it allowing the firefighter to rappel down to safety. Agnon may be using the name here to connote such a last-minute resort.

71. Sitting at her window / Cf. Judges 5:28.

72. Hotel Semiramis / An actual Jaffa hotel at the time, named for legendary queen of Assyria. See Robert Alter's afterword to this volume on the symbolism of the hotel, which becomes a landmark for the final action of the story, bearing the name of "the queen who is a burning image of antiquity's erotic splendor."

72. Because we have no university here / The first institute of higher learning in the Land of Israel was Haifa's Technion – The Israel Institute of Technology, founded in 1912. However the vision of a Jerusalem university mentioned by the school

Balfour speaking at inauguration of Hebrew University (1925)

principal is a reference to the Hebrew University, whose cornerstone was laid in 1918 on Mount Scopus (which overlooks the Temple Mount, as hinted at by the principal), and which began operation in 1925.

73. Blessed be your going out... / Inversion of verse in Deuteronomy 28:6.

77. Zeus / In Greek mythology, Zeus, king of the gods, was also titled Philoxenon (lover of guests), patron god of hospitality and guests.

78. *Beside the brook...* / Opening of a German poem, "The Youth by the Brook" (*"Der Jüngling am Bache"*), by Friedrich von Schiller (1759–1805).

82. Hobbled bird / The Hebrew text reads *dukhifat kfutah*, a bound-up *dukhifat* (bird mentioned in Leviticus 11:19; identified as the hoopoe, a colorful bird with a distinctive crown of feathers). The Talmud mentions this bird, an agent of the mythic Lord of the Sea (*Sara de-Yama*), having committed suicide upon lacking to fulfill a particular "sworn oath" (Gittin 68b and Rashi s.v. *badku*, as per Hullin 63a) – all elements resonating with various symbols in the story.

Dukhifat (Hoopoe)

87. Here, for the time being... / A typically Agnonian indeterminate and ambivalent ending (see the conclusion to *A Simple Story*). There are, however, a number of references to Rechnitz and Shoshanah in other Agnon stories (see for example "Edo and Enam", p. 115 in this volume). In Agnon's *Temol Shilshom*, it's very clear that all Agnon characters of the various Jaffa stories occupy the same literary universe. See there, Book III Chapter 8:1 (p. 415 in the English translation, *Only Yesterday*), which opens: "Isaac got out of bed. He washed his face and hands, but he didn't go to the sea, for it was already noontime, and in those days, we didn't go walking at the sea in the afternoon on hot days, except for Doctor Rekhnitz [sic], who used to hunt for seaweed, *and*

now that he has left for America, you don't see a person at the sea in the afternoon." Jacob, it seems, sets sail for New York after the conclusion of "Betrothed" – whether Shoshanah accompanies him, or what becomes of their life together, is left for the reader to decide.

Edo and Enam

Home of Prof. Gershom Scholem, 28 Abravanel Street, in the Rehavia section of Jerusalem. Agnon was staying here in 1949 when he wrote this story, while Scholem was spending a sabbatical in the United States. "Edo and Enam" was rumored to be inspired by Scholem and his pioneering work in Kabbalah research (a speculation Scholem strongly objected to); the house seems to have served as a model for the setting of the story, which admittedly takes place in a different neighborhood of Jerusalem (Photo by J. Saks).

I

GERHARD GREIFENBACH AND HIS WIFE GERDA, MY TWO GOOD FRIENDS, were just about to go abroad. They hoped to rest a while from the strain of life in our country and visit relatives in the Diaspora. But when I called to wish them well upon their way, it was plain to see that they were really troubled. I hadn't expected anything of the kind. After all, they lived a measured life, enjoyed a steady income, got on well together, and never did anything without first considering it carefully. If they had decided to go on their travels, they had surely managed to eliminate any obstacles and snags. Why then were they so dark and distracted?

We sat together over tea, talking about the countries they were going to visit. A good many lands are no longer accessible, for since the war the world has closed in on us and the countries that admit tourists are fewer in number. Even places which have not barred their doors do not exactly welcome visitors. Still, if a traveler goes about things sensibly, he can find ways of enjoying his trip.

All the time we talked, their anxiety never left them. I began trying to guess at the causes, but could not find any real grounds. These people, I thought to myself, are my friends; indeed I am almost one of the family. After the riots of 1929, when the Arabs had destroyed my home and I had no roof over my head, the Greifenbachs put me up. Again, in the bad times when people who had gone into town could not get back to their homes on account of the curfews suddenly imposed by the British, I had spent several nights at their house. Seeing them so worried, I felt I should ask the reason, but I found some difficulty in framing the question tactfully. I could see Mrs. Greifenbach staring straight ahead of her into the depths of the room. She was like someone looking at a beloved object in order to fix its image so firmly in mind that he will be sure of recognizing it again. Still staring at the room, she remarked, as if to herself, "It's hard to leave and hard to come back.

I only pray that when we get home the doors won't be locked against us and we won't have to go to court with squatters."

Greifenbach made Gerda's words more explicit. "These are fine times," he said, "when we can't even be sure of a roof over our heads. You open the newspaper, only to read about people breaking into other people's homes. You go to the shops and hear of this person or that whose house has been broken into. A man's afraid to go out for a short stroll for fear his house will be grabbed while he is away. And we've all the more reason to be anxious, because our house is so far from any others and a long way out of town. It's true that one room is rented to a Dr. Ginat, but that doesn't help us in the least; most of the time he's away from home, and when we go on our travels the house will be left with no one to guard it."

My heart beat fast as I heard this; not because of the Greifen-bachs, but because they had spoken of Ginat as a real person. Since the time when the name of Ginat became world-famous, I had not come across anyone who could say he actually knew him. Nor had I heard any mention of him, except in connection with his books. And now here he was, staying in this very house where I came and went freely.

Even with his first published article, "Ninety-nine Words of the Edo Language," Ginat had drawn the attention of most of the philologists; when he followed this up with his *Grammar of Edo*, no philologist could afford to ignore him. But what made him truly famous was his discovery of the Enamite Hymns. To discover ninety-nine words of a language whose very name was hitherto unknown is no small achievement, and a greater one still is the compilation of a grammar of this forgotten tongue. But the Enamite Hymns were more: they were not only a new-found link in a chain that bound the beginnings of recorded history to the ages before, but in themselves splendid and incisive poetry. Not for nothing, then, did the greatest scholars come to grips with them, and those who at first had doubted that they were authentic Enamite texts began to compose commentaries on them. One thing, however, surprised me. All these scholars affirmed that the gods of Enam and their priests were male; how was it that they did not catch in the hymns the cadence of a woman's song? On the other hand, I could be mistaken; for I am not, of course, a professional scholar, only a common reader who happens to enjoy anything beautiful that comes his way.

Mrs. Greifenbach could tell that I was excited, but could not tell why. She poured me another cup of tea and repeated what she had been saying before. I held my teacup while my heart pounded; at the same time, I could hear a kind of echo from my very depths. This did not surprise me; ever since the day I had first read the Enamite Hymns that echo had resounded. It was the reverberation of a primeval song passed on from the first hour of history through endless generations.

I held down the turmoil within me and asked, "Is he here?" Even as I said this, I was amazed at my own question. Never had I been inside a house where Ginat had been seen.

"Oh, no," answered Mrs. Greifenbach. "He's not in." Well, I thought, that's clear now. But since they've told me that he has rented a room, they must surely have seen him; and if they've seen him, they may very well have talked to him; and if they've talked to him, perhaps they can tell me something about him. With a great man who shuns publicity and lets nothing be known about himself, even the least bit of information is an unexpected find.

I turned to the Greifenbachs. "May I ask what you know about Ginat?"

"What we know?" answered Greifenbach. "Very little, so little it amounts to less than nothing."

"How did he turn up at your house?"

"That's easily answered," said Greifenbach. "He just rented a room and came to live in it."

"But how did he get here?" I insisted.

"Well, if you want to know the whole story, I can tell you, though there's really nothing to tell."

"Nevertheless, please tell me," I said.

"One afternoon in summer," he went on, "we were out on the veranda having tea, when a man with a walking stick and a knapsack came up and asked if we would rent him a room. We aren't in the habit of renting rooms. Besides, this man didn't so take my fancy that I felt like changing my ways in order to have him as a roomer. On the other hand, I was thinking, We do have a room that has been empty all these years. We've no use for it, and there's a separate entrance, a shower, and so on. Perhaps it would be worthwhile to rent the room, if not for the money's sake, at least to do a good turn to someone who wants to live in this modest neighborhood and is plainly a lover of peace and quiet. This fellow went on to say, 'I promise I won't give you much trouble. I travel about a great deal and only come to Jerusalem for a rest between one journey and the next. I shall not bring in any visitors, either.' I took another look at him and could see that it would be a good thing to rent him the room; not for the reasons he gave, but because by now I rather liked him. In fact, I was surprised at myself for not realizing at once what sort of man he was. I looked across at Gerda and could see that she agreed. So I said to him, 'Very well, the room is yours, on condition that you expect nothing from us; no service or anything at all, except a bed, a table, a chair, and a lamp; and the rent will be such-and-such.' He took out his money and paid down a year's rent, and he has kept to his side of the bargain ever since, making no demands on us. That's all I can tell you, besides what I've seen about him in the literary supplements to the newspapers, which I'm sure you have also read. I dare say you have read his Hymns, too. So have I, a bit here and a bit there, but I still don't see why they are so important. I'm not in the habit of expressing my views about matters on which I'm no expert, but I think I can say this: in every generation, some discovery is made that's regarded as the greatest thing that ever was. Eventually it's forgotten, for meanwhile some new discovery comes to light. No doubt that goes, too, for the discoveries of Dr. Ginat."

I let these remarks pass and returned to the main question, concerning Dr. Ginat himself. "My guess is that Gerda could tell me more," I said.

Mrs. Greifenbach looked at me, surprised that I should credit her with knowledge she didn't possess. She hesitated for a moment, reflected for still another, then said, "I really don't know any more than what Gerhard has told you. There's a separate entrance to the room, we don't have to keep it tidy, and our hard working cleaning woman Grazia, as you know, isn't keen on extra work. Since we gave Ginat the key to his room, I've not been in it, nor have I seen him; after staying here one night, he went off and didn't come back for months."

Having said this, Mrs. Greifenbach began speaking again about their intended journey, throwing in at the same time a sort of complaint. "Your head is so full of our tenant," she said, "that you don't listen to what we are saying."

"Possibly," I answered.

"Don't just say 'possibly,'" she went on, "you must admit that it's absolutely true."

"Heaven forbid that I should contradict you, but please tell me more about Ginat."

"Haven't I already told you, he only stayed one night and went away next morning."

"And didn't you say, too, that he came back? Very well, when he came back what did he do?"

"Do? He closed the door and stayed in his room."

"What was he doing there?"

"Oh, he may have been drawing the pyramids to scale or writing a third part to *Faust.* How do I know?"

I looked hard at her for some time, but she only laughed and said, "I see you want to turn me into a detective."

"No," I answered, "I don't want you to be a detective. I simply want to hear more about Ginat."

I've told you," she said. "Since we gave him his key, I've not spoken to him."

"But what did he do when he came back?"

"I'm sure he did one of the things I've mentioned. Which it was, I've not troubled myself to find out."

"Gerda," said Greifenbach, "just hasn't got that quality women are noted for. She isn't the least bit curious."

Gerda tapped her long, slender fingers on his hairy hands, saying, "*You* have enough of that quality for both of us. So you tell him."

"Who, me??" Greifenbach exclaimed in surprise. "Even I can't tell him about things that never were."

"So you really want me to tell him," said Gerda. "Wasn't it you who said Dr. Ginat had created a girl for himself?"

Greifenbach laughed a long and happy laugh. "Do you know what Gerda's referring to? She's thinking of the legend about the lonely poet – I've forgotten his name – who was said to have created a woman to serve his needs. Are you familiar with that legend?"

"It was Rabbi Solomon Ibn Gabirol," I said, "and if you are interested, this is how the story ends. News of the affair spread about until it reached the king, who gave orders for the woman to be brought before him. The king saw her and fell in love with her, but she ignored him. They went and brought Rabbi Solomon Ibn Gabirol. When he came he showed the king that she was not a real creature, only pieces of wood made up into the likeness of a woman. But what has this legend to do with Dr. Ginat?"

Mrs. Greifenbach said, "One night, Gerhard and I were sitting together reading Goethe when we heard a voice coming from Ginat's room. We knew that Ginat was back from his travels and that he was in there reading. We began our own reading again, and again the voice came through. Gerhard put his book down and said, 'That's a woman's voice.' But it wasn't only the idea of Ginat bringing a woman to his room that surprised us; it was the language she spoke, some strange tongue we had never heard before. Gerhard whispered to me, 'Ginat must have created a girl for himself, and there she is talking to him in her own language.' My dear, that's all I can tell you about Ginat. If you want to know more, ask Gerhard. He loves to make conjectures and treat them as proven facts."

Greifenbach, who had made a hobby of philology, began to speak of the mysteries of language and all the new discoveries in that field. I added something of what I had learned from the literature of the Kabbalah, which in this matter has anticipated academic scholarship. Mrs. Greifenbach interrupted us by saying, "The woman sang, too, in a strange language we knew nothing about. Judging by her voice, I'd say she was sad and bitter. Gerhard, where have you hidden the present our tenant gave you the morning after our anniversary?

What pity you weren't there, my dear. Our wedding, you know, was a very simple affair, but we made up for it with our party ten years after. Don't be lazy, Gerhard; get up and show him what Ginat gave you."

Greifenbach got up, opened an iron box, and took out two parched brown leaves that resembled leaves of old tobacco. He set them before me with pride and watched for my reaction. From the look on his face it was clear that he believed he was exhibiting a rare possession. I glanced at the leaves for a moment and then asked what they were.

"Look again," he said. I looked again but could see nothing except certain strange lines and markings which might be taken, if one were so inclined, for letters of a secret code.

"What is all this?" I insisted.

Greifenbach answered, "I know only what Ginat told me, and what he said was that they are talismans. What kind of talismans he didn't say, but he told me that he has a collection of such things, and these leaves are duplicates and come from a far-off country. It's a pity they have no power against burglars."

"Perhaps," said Gerda, "those that Ginat kept for himself do have that power."

Greifenbach lit his pipe and sat silent, as if preoccupied with his own thoughts. After a while he knocked out the ash and took a cigarette. He lit up and went on, "You see, whatever we find to talk about leads us back to our worries about the house. As for the squatters, it's even possible that right is on their side. A young fellow, let us say, comes back after the war. He needs a roof over his head and can't find one. What's he to do but break in somewhere? Let me tell you something. One Saturday evening I was standing at a bus stop. The bus was full up and passengers were still pressing in. The driver sounded his horn and drove off. All the people left behind stood about miserably as they waited for a second bus. But, of course, it never came; the more passengers there are, the fewer the buses, as is always the case in Jerusalem. A couple were standing together, a young fellow and a girl. The girl was looking at him with passionate longing. 'Günther,' she said, 'it's over a year since we were married and we've still not spent a single night alone together.' The fellow squeezed his young wife's hand, sucked his lips in and was silent with grief and anger. Günther and his wife haven't found a home for themselves. They live apart, wherever they happen to be. The landlords make difficulties about their visiting one another, hoping that they will get tired of their rooms and leave them, because meanwhile the number of people wanting apartments has increased and the number of rooms available has become less, and if they leave, the landlords can raise the rent. They meet each other in cafés and amusement places and separate to go back to their rooms at the opposite ends of the town, all because they have no place where they can live together. So now you know why we are so scared about our home. In fact, we got into such a state that one night Gerda woke me up because she thought someone was walking on the roof."

"You are always telling tales about me," said Mrs. Greifenbach. "Why don't you tell him what *you* said?"

"I said nothing. I don't remember saying anything."

"Do you want me to remind you?" said Gerda.

Gerhard laughed heartily. "And if I don't want you to, does that mean you won't tell him?"

"If it weren't so funny," said Gerda, "I wouldn't repeat it. Do you know what this master mind had to say? He said, in these very words, 'It must be the girl Ginat created, taking a stroll on the roof.'"

Greifenbach laid down his cigarette, took up his pipe again, and remarked to me, "Do you really believe I said that?"

"Who wouldn't believe a lovely girl like Gerda?"

Mrs. Greifenbach laughed. "A lovely girl, indeed," she said, "whose wedding canopy has been pressing on her head for ten years now!"

"Have you two really been married for ten years already?"

"Those leaves," said Gerda, "which Ginat gave to Gerhard were his present on our tenth anniversary. If they came into just anybody's hands he'd probably break them up as tobacco for his pipe. He wouldn't know there was magic in them. To tell the truth, we wouldn't have known either if we hadn't heard it from Ginat; and we believe him, because he's quite without guile. Well, tomorrow we start on our travels, and I don't know whether I should feel glad or sorry."

Without thinking about it much, I said to Gerda, "You've no need to feel sorry. I'll take it upon me to keep an eye on your house, and if I think it necessary, I'll stay here for two or three nights."

The Greifenbachs were delighted at this offer. "Now we can travel with an easy mind," they said.

"Surely you don't have to thank me," I added.

"Really, it's I who ought to thank you; your house is a wonderful place for sleep, as I learned on curfew nights."

My remark brought back to mind that troubled time, when people who went into the city could not get home again because the Mandate government had suddenly proclaimed a curfew. Anyone out on the Street who lived away from the center and couldn't find shelter in town would be taken by the police and locked up in jail for the night. His family, not knowing where he had disappeared to, would be worried to death. And this had led to other oppressive decrees against us, decrees which at the time seemed to be in the very nature of life in this country. So we talked on about the curfew nights. Yet, evil and oppressive as they were, some little good came of them. People were obliged to stay at home and as a result gave thought to their wives and children, which they had not been accustomed to doing when they spent their evenings at assemblies, councils, meetings and the like, all of which estrange a man from himself and, needless to say, from his family. You might even say that public affairs benefited; with fewer meetings and debates things worked out in their own way, and in spite of it all turned out for the best. Another positive result of the curfew nights was that many bachelors, compelled to stay indoors, came to know the daughters of the house and ended up marrying them.

So we sat and talked, the Greifenbachs and I, until I said it was time for me to go. Greifenbach gave me the key of the house and showed me all its entrances and exits. Soon afterwards I parted from him and his wife and went on my way.

II

One day at sunset I went out to get myself some bread and olives. My wife and children had gone away to Gederah, and I was left to provide for myself. Carrying my bread and olives, I strolled about among the shops. I had no desire to go home, since no one was there and there was nothing I especially wished to do at the day's end. Walking on aimlessly, letting my feet carry me where they wished, I found I had come to the valley where the Greifenbach's house stood. In the stillness that fills the valleys of Jerusalem at sunset all manner of blessings abide. It is as if the valleys were cut off from the settled land around them; as if they contained in their depths the whole world. And this valley especially is ringed with a crown of trees through which beneficent vapors flow, keeping it free from the taint of malign airs. I said to myself, Since I am here, I shall go and see how things stand at the Greifenbachs' house; and since I have the key in my pocket, I may as well go inside.

I went in, put on the light, and walked about from room to room. The four pleasant rooms and their equally agreeable contents were all in good order, as if the mistress of the house had just given them her attention. Yet a month had already passed since the Greifenbachs left home. Truly, when a house has a good mistress it remains well kept even though she is far away.

Just then I was neither hungry nor thirsty, only tired. I put out all the lights, opened the window, and sat down to rest. Out of the secret places of the night, silence came and wrapped itself around me until I could see and touch the tranquility. I made up my mind to spend the night there and so keep my promise to the Greifenbachs. I rose from my seat and lit the table lamp. Then I picked up a book to read in bed by a lamp already at the bedside, glad that I would not need to shift any article in someone else's house. Actually, so long as I held the key, I had the right to regard myself as in my own home; but the sense of strangeness we feel on such occasions makes us forget our privileges.

I sat in Greifenbach's chair and reflected. Just now, while I am staying in their house, perhaps they are looking in vain for a place to spend the night; or if they have found one, it is not the kind they are accustomed to. Why should they have left their beautifully furnished home to wander about in foreign parts? What reason, indeed, have all those who leave their homes and drift from place to place? Is it a first law of our experience or a mocking illusion that, as the ancient proverb has it, "Your happiness is where you are not"?

I took off my shoes, undressed, picked up my book, put out the table lamp and lit the one by the bed. I lay down and opened the book. I could feel myself dozing off, while an idea of sorts seemed to be thinking itself out on its own. Strange, I thought, that I, who on other nights can't get to sleep even after midnight, should now feel suddenly drowsy before the night has properly set in. I put the book down, switched off the light, turned to face the wall and closed my eyes. I told myself in silent speech: Here in this house, where not a soul in the world knows of your presence, you can sleep as long as you like and no one will come to seek you.

All around me was stillness and repose, such as one finds in the valleys of Jerusalem, which the good Lord hid away for lovers of tranquility. The Greifenbachs had good reason to be concerned for their home: if any squatter were to break in, no one hereabouts would be aware of it. Little by little the run of my thoughts came to a halt, until nothing remained but the dim sensation that all my limbs were locked in sleep.

Suddenly I heard a sound of scratching and awoke. Since I had put my bread and olives away in a tin box, I was not afraid that mice might get at them; but I was afraid that mice might damage the carpet, the clothes or books, or those leaves that Ginat had given to Greifenbach. I pricked up my ears and realized that the sound was not made by a mouse, but by a man who was fumbling at the outside door. If it's not a housebreaker, I thought, then it must be Dr. Ginat, who has come home and is trying the wrong door. I'll open up for him, and so I'll see him face to face.

I got out of bed and opened the door. Someone was outside, groping for the bell. I pressed the switch, put on the light, and then – words failed me. After all, I had not told a soul that I would be spending the night at the Greifenbachs', indeed, I myself hadn't known that I would be here, how then could Gabriel Gamzu have known my whereabouts?

"Is it you, Mr. Gamzu?" I called. "Wait a moment while I put on some clothes."

I went back and dressed, wondering why this visitor was here. He was not acquainted with either the owner of the house or his wife. Greifenbach was not looking for books in Hebrew, even less for manuscripts and first editions. The little Hebrew he knew had been learned with difficulty. Although he prided himself on his sound knowledge of the language and its grammar, all this amounted to was some biblical grammar he had studied in Gesenius' textbook on the structure of Hebrew. His wife managed better than he, for although her grammar was an amateur affair and she knew nothing of Gesenius, she could get on in Hebrew with her cleaning woman Grazia, and with the street traders too. All the same, Hebrew books were none of her concern. So the question still stood, what had brought Gamzu here? I had to conclude that he was here on my account. Gamzu knew that he was always welcome, to me as to all his friends and acquaintances, because he was a scholar, had seen the world, had voyaged to distant lands, and reached places where no traveler had been before. From these far-off parts he had brought back poems by authors about whom nothing was known and manuscripts and first editions of whose very existence we had been ignorant. But now he no longer traveled at all; he stayed at home with his wife. This man, so used to making journeys, had become in his prime the attendant of a sick wife who, it was said, had been bedridden since their wedding night. Whether or not the story was true, it was certainly a fact that he had a sick wife at home, that there was no earthly cure for her, and that her husband had to nurse her, wash her, feed her and attend to her every need. Nor was she grateful for his self-sacrifice, but would beat him and bite him and tear his clothes. Because of this he went about his business at night, being ashamed to show himself in the street by day with torn clothing and bruised face. Now he had come to me. And why had he come? He had saved twelve pounds to purchase a place for his wife in a nursing home; he was afraid to carry the money about on him in case he should spend it, and so he had left it with me. On the day he did so I had gone on a trip to the Dead Sea region and left the money behind at home. Thieves had broken in and robbed my house and taken Gamzu's money. I had sent him a message not to worry about it; all the same, he had come to hear from me directly whether I was really prepared to repay him what had been stolen. And since he had not been able to find me at home, he had come to see me here. This was my conjecture. I was later to see that it was wrong; Gamzu had not come on account of the money, but for another reason.

III

Having put on some clothes, I returned to Gamzu and said, "You've come for your money?"

He gazed at me woefully with an uncertain look in his eyes, imploring in a broken voice, "Please let me in."

I showed him into the house and offered him a chair. He looked around in all directions and deliberated for a while. At last he stammered out, "My wife." After another pause he added, "I went home and my wife wasn't there."

"So what do you intend to do?" I asked.

"Forgive me," he said, "for suddenly bursting in on you. Just imagine: I came home after the evening service at the synagogue to get my wife settled for the night and found the bed empty. I went off in search of her. 'Going to the south, turning to the north, turning, turning goes the wind, and again to its circuits the wind returns.' Suddenly I found myself in this valley without knowing how I came to be here. I saw a house; I felt drawn to enter it. I knew there was no point in doing this, but I did so just the same. It's good that I found you. Let me sit here for a short while and then I'll go away."

"Pardon me for asking, Mr. Gamzu," I said. "I have heard that your wife is bedridden."

"Bedridden she is," Gamzu replied.

"Then how is it that you found the bed empty? If she can't move, how did she get out of bed and go outside?"

He whispered, "She's a sleepwalker."

I sat for a while without speaking. Then I repeated his words in the form of a question, whispering back, "A sleepwalker?"

"Yes."

I looked at him as a man might who has heard a report and does not know what to make of it. Perceiving this, he said, "Every night when the moon is full, my wife gets up from bed and walks wherever the moon leads her."

I could not keep myself from saying reproachfully, "And don't you lock the door?"

Gamzu smiled slyly. "I lock the door."

"If so," I said, "how can she get out?"

"Even if I hung seven locks upon the door, and locked every one with seven keys, and threw each key into one of the seven seas of the Land of Israel, my wife would find them all and open the door and go walking."

I sat on, saying nothing, and he too sat in silence. At last I said, "Since when have you known that she is in that condition? I mean, that she's a sleepwalker?"

He clutched his forehead, dug his thumbs into his temples, and said, "Since when have I known that she is a sleepwalker? I have known since the day I met her."

I was silent again, but not for long. "Nevertheless," I said, "this did not keep you from marrying her."

He took off his hat, brought out a small skullcap and put it on, paused, and asked, "What were you saying?"

I repeated my words.

He smiled and said, "Nevertheless it did not pre-vent me from marrying her. On the contrary, when I saw her for the first time poised on a rock at the top of a mountain which not every man could climb, with the moon lighting up her face while she sang, '*Yiddal, yiddal, yiddal, vah, pah, mah,*' I said to myself, If she is not one of the angels of the Divine Presence who have union with the angels of the Divine Being, she must be one of the twelve constellations of the Zodiac, and none other than the constellation Virgo. I went to her father's home and said, 'I wish to marry your daughter.' He answered me, 'My son, you know of Gemulah's condition and yet you wish to marry her?' I said, 'The All-Merciful will be merciful to us.' He looked up to the sky, addressing the Holy One, 'Master of the World, if this man who comes from afar is filled with mercy towards her, how much more so will you, who are so near, show mercy to us.' Next day he called me and said, 'Come with me.'

I went with him until we reached a mountain, the highest of the range of steep mountains that raised themselves up to heaven. I climbed with him, leaping with him from crag to crag, until he stood by a perpendicular rock. He looked about him in all directions. When he knew that no one could see us, he bent down and dug beneath the rock and lifted one stone. A cave opened up and he went inside. When he came out, he was holding an earthenware jar. 'Let us go back,' he said. On the way back, he opened the jar and showed me a bundle of dry leaves unlike any I had ever seen; and on them were the strange characters of a script unlike any that I knew; and the color of the characters, that is, the color of the ink in which they were written, was not like any color we know. At first sight I should have said that the scribe had mixed gold, azure and purple with all the primary colors of the rainbow and written with them. But as I stood gazing, the colors altered before my eyes and changed into the tints of sea-weeds drawn from the depths, such weeds as Dr. Rechnitz drew up from the sea near Jaffa. Then again, they were like the silver strands we observe on the moon. I stared at the leaves, at the characters, at Gemulah's father. At that moment he seemed as if transported to another world. And then it became increasingly clear that what at first sight had seemed an illusion was the truth itself. If you ask me what it all meant, I can give you no answer. For my part it was clear, crystal clear, even though I wonder now how I am able to say this. And if I have no words to describe the experience, yet it was more distinct than anything one can explain in words. At that moment I had neither speech nor power to ask any question; and the cause of this was not the leaves or the characters on them, but the ecstatic state of Gemulah's father. As for the characters, all the colors which I had seen before faded later and underwent a complete change, but I have no clear knowledge of how the characters came to shed their colors and when this change came about. As I stood marveling, Gemulah's father replaced the leaves in the jar and spoke to me simply, with these words: 'They are plants of the earth, and they have been given power to influence the upper air.'

"A year later, on the night before our wedding, he said, 'You will remember those plants which I showed you on the mountain.

You know what they are.' He stooped and whispered in my ear, 'There is a magic in them; what kind of magic I do not know. I do know that it has power to influence the atmosphere that surrounds the moon, and the moon itself. I now give you all these plants, and as long as they remain in your keeping you may control Gemulah's steps so that she will not go astray. Up to now, I have not taken them from the place where they were concealed. And why? Because, so long as Gemulah is calm and sheltered and wrapped up in her own wholeness, they serve no purpose. Now that the time has come for love and union with her husband, when she must draw upon her husband's strength, she is subject to a different influence and another mode of being. So, when the nights of the full moon come, take these plants and set them in the window facing the door, and hide them so that no man will notice them, and I assure you that if Gemulah leaves the house she will return to you before the moon returns to her proper sphere.'"

I said to Gamzu, "Tonight you forgot to follow all your father-in-law's instructions."

"I did not forget."

"Well then, how did it happen?"

Gamzu spread out his two empty hands and said, as if to himself, "Gabriel, your magic has gone."

"You mean it has lost its power over her?"

"Not at all," he answered. "It has gone from me."

"Has your wife rooted it out?" I asked.

"Not at all," he said. "I am the cause. I sold it. By mistake, I sold it. There was a gathering of scholars here, many scholars from all over the world came together in Jerusalem. Some came to my house to buy books and manuscripts. As they turned them over hurriedly, one man rummaging among the books I had set aside and another looking at those which his colleague had taken, in the midst of all this confusion those charms got mixed up in a heap of miscellaneous manuscripts and I sold them without knowing to whom. I don't remember, though I should have, for I can remember every manuscript I sold, but not this; and the money I got is the penalty I am paying, twelve pounds, which I left with you to buy Gemulah a place in the home for incurables."

Gamzu clutched his brow and pressed his temples. Then he rubbed his blind eye with one finger; for Gamzu had a blind eye, and when he was overcome by his thoughts he would rub it until it turned as red as healthy flesh. He wiped his finger and looked across at me as if he wanted me to say something. What can I say to him, I thought; I shall say nothing. So I sat facing him in silence. Again he spoke.

"Sometimes I think that Gemulah knows the man who bought it; that he is the *Hakham* from Jerusalem who appeared in her region when I was away in Vienna. And for this I have two pieces of evidence. First, all that same day she sang her *yiddal, yiddal, yiddal* song, a thing she had never done all the time she was here. Secondly, she began to speak the language they use in her parts, a thing she had never done since she left her country. I am sure that the man who bought the talismans brought this about; when she saw him she remembered the times when she lived in her own region and that same man had been a visitor. But then he was dressed like a Jerusalem sage; for anyone who visits those parts dresses that way so that the holiness of the city may protect him from the Gentiles."

Again Gamzu rubbed his blind eye, which seemed to be smiling between his fingers, as if mocking his distress, as if winking for me to laugh at this man who had sold an article on which his life and that of his wife depended. But I did not feel like deriding him. Rather, I was sorry for him. The thought suddenly came into my head that Dr. Ginat was the man who had acquired Gamzu's talismans; for had I not heard from Greifenbach that Ginat had a collection of magic articles and had given him some duplicates? I asked Gamzu, "About those charms, what material are they written on? Is it paper or parchment?"

Gamzu answered, "Neither paper nor parchment nor vellum; as I told you before, the charms are inscribed on leaves."

I correlated the times and saw that it was impossible for Ginat to have been the purchaser; indeed, that scholars' convention had taken place after the tenth anniversary of the Greifenbachs' marriage. And even if it had taken place before, was it conceivable that a European like Ginat would dress himself up as a Jerusalem sage, and be able to pass himself off as such?

Gamzu had read much, and studied much, and served many scholars; he had traveled through half the world. Truly there was not a community of Jews in which Gamzu had not been. Besides manuscripts and early printed books, he had brought back from every place he had been traditional tales and customs, wise men's sayings and proverbs, and stories of travelers. Whatever occurred, he would tell of similar occurrences as though recent events took place merely as the occasion for him to recall earlier ones; or he would pick up a word from those being spoken, and speak on it. Even now, he passed on from his immediate distress over the charms to an account of the way in which charms operate.

There sat Gamzu and rolled himself a cigarette and talked about the magic properties of charms, whose virtue is superior to that of drugs; for the drugs we find mentioned in ancient books cannot for the most part be relied on, since the nature of man has changed and with these changes the effect of medicines has altered. But charms have undergone no change and still retain their first nature and condition, because they are yoked together with the stars, and the stars remain just as they were on the day when they were first hung in the firmament. And their influence is observed on all creatures, and especially on man; for according to the star under which he is born, such is a man's character and his fate. As it is said in the Talmud, "All depends upon one's star," and it is said, "Our star makes us wise, or makes us rich." The maladies of man likewise depend upon the stars, for the Holy One, blessed be He, gave the stars their power to work upon the lower orders of creation, whether for good or ill. The earth too is altered according to the stars, as Ibn Ezra put it in his commentary on Exodus, "For the regions of the earth change according to whatever star is above them"; and he also wrote, "And those who have the wisdom of the stars know this." Yet we must not attribute to the stars in themselves any power or purpose, for all their power and purpose stems from that of their Maker and Creator, who keeps them employed. And what need, if one can so phrase it, has the Holy One of stars, except that, as Proverbs says, "The Lord hath made everything for His own sake." *Le-ma'anehu, for His own sake.* This last word should be derived from *ma'aneh,* meaning song and praise, as in the verse, "sing out - *anu* - to the Lord in praise." And this is just what David said in his psalm: "The heavens declare the glory of God and the firmament declares His handiwork." All that the Holy One created was made for the sake of Israel, that they might know how to give honor to the Holy One and how to recount His praise, and that the prophecy might be fulfilled, "This people that I have created, they will declare My praise." And the stars, like the angels, are half of them male and half of them female, in heaven as it is on earth, male and female; even so are the letters of the word "heaven" equal numerically to those of "male and female." And this being so, they yearn for each other, in heaven as on earth; and thus the way a man and woman are drawn each to the other is in accordance with their stars. What, then, gave the children of Benjamin such assurance, when they seized in the vineyards, each man a wife from the daughters of Shiloh? Were they not apprehensive that they might be unsuitably matched? But they knew that in the time to come the Temple would be built on the heights of their land, and that all Israel would have a share in it. For this very reason the color of the flag of Benjamin resembles the colors of all the rest of the tribes, and accordingly they were sure that the women they seized were their destined mates.

IV

As often happens with ideas, which you may develop as far as you wish or break away from at any time you please, so with Gamzu's account of the workings of charms and the functioning of stars: he went on until he chose to stop, and then began to tell me of his travels.

"If you wish to see Jews from the days of the Mishnah," said Gamzu, "go to the city of Amadia. Forty families of Israel live there, all God-fearing and true to the faith. They rise each morning to say their prayers; but they do not know how to pray, except for the verse 'Hear O Israel' and the response 'Amen.' They do not put on *Tefillin,* save for the rabbi and one old man. At times of prayer they sit in silence, and when the prayer leader says the blessings, they devoutly reply, 'Amen.' When the service brings them to the recital of 'Hear O Israel,' they shiver and quake, and recite it throughout in fear and dread, with trembling and terror, like men whose time has come to sacrifice their souls for God. And in the neighborhood of Amadia, shepherds move about, men of great stature with long hair; they sleep with their herds in clefts of the rocks, and do not know the laws of the Torah, not the least iota, and do not come to pray even on Rosh Hashanah. To them and to those like them that passage in the Mishnah refers: 'The case of a person who was passing behind the synagogue and happened to hear the sound of the Shofar.' Once a year a *Hakham* from Babylon comes to circumcise the boys who were born during that year." "Is your wife of this people?" I asked him.

"My wife is not one of them. My wife is from another region, from the mountains. At first, her ancestors were settled beside the good springs, where the pasture was also good. But their neighbors made war on them, and they retaliated and drove them back. Because of their great might some of their troops advanced into the lands of the Gentiles, for they misconceived the text: 'And to Gad he said, Blessed be he who enlarges Gad; he dwells as a lioness, and tears the arm, yea, the crown of the head.' For they have a tradition that they are of the tribe of Gad, but they did not know that the blessing refers only to the time when they lived in the Land of Israel, not to their exile in the lands of other peoples. All the Gentiles gathered together against them and defeated them and killed many and captured many as slaves. Those who were left took to the high mountains and settled there. They remain there still, and have no fear of the Gentiles; but once every few years collectors come to gather taxes from them. Those who are so disposed pay them, the others take up their weapons and hide in the mountains until the tax collectors have gone. Sometimes it happens that a man who has fled does not return, because he has been made a prey of the eagles who attack and tear him with their talons. And all this time they have looked forward to their return to the Land of Israel, as was promised them by God through Moses our Teacher, peace upon him, who said that they would all return, according to the text: 'Gad, a troop shall overcome him, but he shall overcome at the last.' All his troops shall regain their inheritance, which they took up beyond the Jordan, and no man of them shall be missing. Moreover they will come back with great possessions, as is written in the Aramaic Targum: 'And with ample riches they shall return to their land.'"

Gamzu went on to relate how when he first came upon them they were dejected, with many sick at heart because of their long exile and long-deferred hope. But Gevariah ben Ge'uel, his father-in-law, is remembered for good, for he read to them from the Midrash and the Jerusalem Targum, which they have in its complete text, and which he translated into their language, and so gave them new heart, till they began to remember all the promises and assurances given us by the Holy One concerning the time of the Messiah.

Gamzu continued, "Gevariah ben Ge'uel, my father-in-law, was a mighty man. His face was the face of a lion, his strength was that of a bull, and he was light-footed as an eagle in flight. High praises of God were in his mouth and a two-edged sword in his hand. He led his people in prayer, and he forged their weapons of war. He also healed the sick, wrote charms, and taught betrothed maidens the marriage dances and songs. For this he would take no fee; all his works were done for the sake of heaven. And Gemulah his daughter was his mainstay. She was accomplished in all their songs, those that they had once sung when they dwelt by the springs and also those of the mountains.

"If you had seen my father-in-law Gevariah when he stood on the peak of a rock, a sky-blue turban on his head, his complexion and beard set off by his flowing hair, his dark eyes shining like two suns, his feet bare and the color of gold, his big toes striking the towering rock while he raised a song from the depths as he led his troops onward and Gemulah his daughter sang at full pitch and between twenty-two and twenty-seven maidens danced, all of them beautiful and high born, then you would have seen a likeness of the festive days of ancient Israel, when the daughters of Israel went out to dance in the vineyards."

And how did Gamzu come to their land? "I had gone in search of manuscripts. I sailed the sea routes and walked for forty days in the wilderness. A sandstorm arose. But I failed to lay my head to the ground after the manner of those who cross the desert, who cover their heads when a sandstorm strikes, and when the storm has blown over stand up unhurt. The sand got into my eyes and blinded me; there was darkness all around me.

The leader of the caravan saw my distress, and after some days brought me to a settled region, and to the house of a certain man, saying, 'He is of your people.' That man was Gevariah ben Ge'uel. He prepared charms and medicines for me, and his daughter Gemulah tended me as I lay sick.

"Gemulah was then about twelve years old, and her gracious bearing and lovely voice were the most beautiful things in the world. Even when she spoke of commonplace things, saying, for instance, 'Your bandage has slipped, Gabriel,' or 'Look down while I put ointment in your eye,' my spirit rejoiced as if odes had been chanted to me. And when she sang, her voice stirred the heart like that of the bird Grofit, whose song is sweeter than that of any creature on earth. At first I had difficulty in understanding their speech, even when they spoke to me in the Holy Tongue, because their Hebrew has more full vowels and fewer elided syllables than ours and they pronounce words differently. Their speech rhythms are strange, too, so that I was unable to distinguish between their Hebrew and the language they spoke among themselves, a language that no outsider has heard. Gemulah and her father had yet another language. Often I would find them sitting in the twilight, a white kid lying in Gemulah's lap and a bird hovering over the old man's head, while they conversed, sometimes in a leisurely way and sometimes in haste, sometimes cheerfully and sometimes with an expression of fear. I would listen to them but not understand a word, until Gemulah revealed to me that this was an invented language which they had made up for their own pastime. Since the day Gemulah was torn from her native soil all that speech has disappeared from her lips, nor does she express herself in any song, save on the nights when the moon is full and she takes her walks, singing as she goes. But on the day when I sold the magic text, she spoke in that language and let her lovely voice be heard in song. And in the evening she said, 'I want to eat *kavanim*.' This is a kind of flat cake which they bake on live coals. Now I must go and see if my wife has come back."

Gamzu took off his skullcap, placed his hat on his head, and stood up. But he had not got as far as the door when he turned back and began to pace about the room, his arms folded behind him, the fingers of his left hand fluttering nervously. After a little while he said, "I can't understand why I came here, especially since I saw no light and didn't know you were in the house; but certainly there is some reason for my coming, and even if I don't know the reason, that doesn't remove it. Who lives here?"

"A certain Dr. Greifenbach," I said.

"And where is he?"

"He has gone abroad with his wife. Do you know them?"

"I do not know them," said Gamzu. "Is Greifenbach a doctor of medicine?"

"He is a doctor who has left his profession. Why do you ask?"

"Apart from these people, who else is here?"

"You and I. Before they went on their travels, I promised the Greifenbachs that I would keep an eye on their house. They were worried about squatters, since there are so many of them now among the soldiers back from the war. Tonight I have kept my promise and come to stay here."

Gamzu pricked up his ears. "And is no one else lodging in the house?"

"There is someone else," I said, "who is not at home. Why do you ask?"

Gamzu blushed and said nothing. After a while he asked again, "What is the name of that lodger?"

I told him.

"Can he be the famous Dr. Ginat?" asked Gamzu.

"Do you know him?"

"I don't know him, though I have heard of his books. But I haven't read them. I don't look at books that are less than four hundred years old."

"Ginat's books," I replied, "go back four thousand years and more."

Gamzu smiled. "I am looking at the vessel and not what it contains."

Smiling in turn, I said, "Well, then, in another four hundred years you'll be looking at Ginat's books."

"If in my third or fourth incarnation I am still interested in books," said Gamzu, "it's quite possible that I shall."

"Two or three incarnations," I replied, "are all a man goes through, according to the words of Scripture: 'And it is said, unto three transgressions of Israel, yea, four, I shall not reverse it.' No man of Israel passes through this world more than two or three times, unless he is obliged to fulfill some precept he has omitted from the six hundred and thirteen in the Torah; in which case he may even go through a thousand cycles of life, with reference to which it is said: 'He commanded it unto the thousandth generation.' But otherwise this is not so, yet you speak of a fourth incarnation."

"It was a slip on my part," said Gamzu. "You know my opinion, that no Jew is capable of saying anything for which the Bible gives no support, and especially that which is contrary to the plain meaning of the text. And do not answer me with those Bible critics who turn the words of the living God upside down. This they have learned from Gentile scholars, but in the depths of their heart they know that no text of Scripture has any other meaning than that which has been passed down to us by tradition. Yes, and the Hasidic leaders, they too twist the words of the Holy Writ; but the truly righteous who study the Torah for its own sake, with the intention of serving heaven, these only have the right to interpret scripture beyond its simple meaning. But as for the Bible critics who have not the merit of studying the Torah for its own sake, their teaching is perverted in accordance with the emptiness of their own spirit. So you say that Ginat lodges here. Do you know him?"

"I do not know him," I said, "and I doubt if I shall get to know him. He hides away from people, and even the owners of the house do not see him."

"It is a good sign when people don't know a scholar. I like scholars who don't show up in every place and make themselves into a public spectacle. Let me tell you something. I once came to London and informed a certain scholar there that I had brought manuscripts with me. He got busy and came along with two escorts, a journalist and a photographer. He took all the material I showed him and sat himself down in the pose of a great savant looking at his books, while the photographer stood there taking pictures. Two or three days later, someone showed me a newspaper. I looked at it and saw a face framed by books printed alongside praises of that scholar, who, it seemed, had discovered precious works that were quite unknown until he brought them to light. What do you think of that?"

I said to Gamzu, "I think as you do."

Gamzu looked at me with an expression of annoyance. "You don't know what I think, so why say you think as I do?"

"Very well. I don't think as you do."

"Are you making fun of me?" he asked.

"Not of you," I answered, "but of that scholar, and of those like him, who waste their energies in trying to prop up their reputation. Whereas if they concentrated on their work, possibly they would become more famous."

"They would not become more famous."

"If so, they are right in behaving as they do."

"I must go," said Gamzu.

It was near midnight when he left, and I walked with him part of the way. The moon was full and the entire city glistened like the moon. If you have ever seen such a night, you will not find it strange that somnambulists leave their beds to go out and wander with the moon. When we reached the Georgian Quarter at the Damascus Gate I parted from Gamzu, expressing the hope that he would find his wife. He took out a handkerchief, wiped his eyes, and said, "God willing."

"If you want to get in touch with me," I said, "you will find me at my home. I mean to go back in the morning."

V

I returned to the Greifenbachs' house and went back to bed. Sleep came quickly, and I knew nothing until I was roused by the sound of train wheels. The train reached Garmisch and stopped there. The door of the compartment opened and there was a view of high mountains and streams; I could hear a voice singing *yiddal, yiddal, yiddal, vah, pah, mah.* I was drawn by the voice and wanted to follow it. The door was shut against me. The moon came out and covered me with her light. I smiled at her with one eye and she smiled back with a grin that covered all her face.

But there was no train. I was in bed at the Greifenbachs'. I turned over to one side and pulled the blanket over my eyes, because the moon was shining on my face. I was thinking of how the world has shut itself in so that none of us can go where he wishes, except for the moon, that wanders over all the earth, singing *yiddal, yiddal, yiddal, vah, pah, mah.*

After lunching at a restaurant in town, I had gone home to get on with my work. But when I broke off to make myself some coffee, I found there was not a drop of water in the tap. I went up to the roof and inspected the water tanks. They had become overheated in the sun and the water at the bottom of the tanks was barely an inch deep. Jerusalem, a dry place, was at that time badly in need of water. I left my work behind and went over to the Greifenbachs', for their house has a cistern, such as you find in the older houses of Jerusalem that were built when people drank rain water.

They had lived through many lives, the houses of Jerusalem. There is not one without a long story to it, especially the first ones to be built outside the walls. The Greifenbachs' house was no exception.

About seventy years ago, there came to the land a grandee of the grandees of Gallipoli, Signor Gamaliel Giron, to spend the close of his life in the Holy City. He found no house to suit his needs, for the Jewish population was confined to the old courtyards within the walls, and every courtyard was inhabited by many families, and each family was a large one. So he bought himself two thousand square cubits of land outside the city, below the Damascus Gate, and built there a spacious house and planted a garden. And because the house was a long way from the populated area, with no synagogue in the neighborhood, he set apart one room as a private chapel and hired men to come and make up a Minyan for prayer. On his demise he bequeathed the house to the charitable society *Gomlei Hasadim.* In time those in charge of the society's finances became pressed for money to pay the army tax, and mortgaged the house. The house remained under a mortgage for some years, they were unable to redeem it, and accordingly it was sold by those who had advanced the loan.

The house was sold to a German named Gotthold Gänseklein, who was head of the sect of Guardians, who had seceded from the sect of the *Gemeinschaft der Gerechten,* founded in the city of Gerlitz by Gottfried Greilich. Gänseklein, his wife and his mother-in-law lived in this house, and here he would hold prayer meetings and preach concerning the three true guards for redeeming the body and extending the limits of the soul. One night a quarrel occurred between Gänseklein's wife and her mother. The wife bit her mother's nose in order to disgrace her before the husband. People came to hear of this affair and Gänseklein was obliged to quit the country for shame.

Three Georgian brothers-in-law, who supported themselves by manufacturing Gouda cheese, now bought the house and made their cheese there. The Great War broke out, and Gamal Pasha expelled them from the country, because they were suspected of Zionism, the Star of David having been found stamped upon the cheese. After the war the Council of Delegates rented the house for their fellow member Georg Gnadenbrod. The house was repaired, the refuse heap cleared away, the garden replanted and the estate fenced in. Mr. Gnadenbrod had scarcely taken possession when his wife, Gnendlein, put her foot down and said that she did not wish to live in Jerusalem. They returned to Glasgow and the house was made into business offices. Then came the earthquake, which damaged the building and weakened the roof. For some years the house stood untenanted until Gerhard Greifenbach rented it and repaired it and decorated it and installed electric lighting and plumbing and other modern improvements. He and his wife had lived there until they felt a longing to go abroad and rest a while from the strain of life in our country, and I was asked to keep an eye on the house lest squatters break in and take possession. And now I was spending two nights there.

Cut off from the settled area, the house stood alone in the valley, surrounded by its garden gleaming in the light of the moon. And in that moonlight the garden and all that was in it, every tree, every shrub, seemed detached and unconcerned with its neighbor's affairs. Only the moon made no distinctions and shone impartially on all.

I stood at the window and looked out at the garden. Every tree, every shrub slept its deep sleep; but among the trees movements could be heard. If these were not the footsteps of Ginat returned from his journey, perhaps they were Gabriel Gamzu's. When I had gone along with him on the previous night I had asked him to let me know how his wife was; he had come back, then, to tell me. Or perhaps it was not Gamzu; after all, it could be anybody.

But that pure, perfect moonlight did not deceive me. It was none other than Gamzu walking this way. I went and opened the door and showed him into the room. Gamzu picked a chair and sat down. He took out some paper and rolled himself a cigarette. He put the cigarette to his lips, lit it and sat there smoking, paying no attention to me as I waited to hear if he had found his wife. I was annoyed, and in my annoyance said nothing.

"You don't ask me about my wife," said Gamzu.

"If you've anything to tell me, let me hear."

"Indeed I have something to tell you. Isn't there an ashtray?"

I went and brought him an ashtray. He groped about to deposit the stub of his cigarette. Then he looked at me with his healthy eye, wiped his ailing eye, rubbed his palm against his beard, licked his palm with the tip of his tongue, and remarked, "I thought I had burnt myself with my cigarette, but now I see that I have been bitten by a mosquito. You have mosquitoes in the house."

"Perhaps there is a mosquito here and perhaps there isn't a mosquito here. Who would notice a mosquito when he is honored by the presence of a dear guest like you?"

I do not know how Gamzu took this. What he said was, "I found her! I found her! Found her in bed fast asleep!"

It would be interesting, I thought, to know how Gamzu came to find his wife. But I shall not ask him outright. If he tells me, well and good; if not, I shall do without the information, rather than have him think that I am prying into his affairs. A few moments went by in which he said nothing; it looked as if he had put the whole matter out of his mind. Suddenly he passed his hand over his brow like a man stirring himself from sleep, and proceeded to tell me how he had come home, opened the door and looked into the bedroom without expecting to find anything. All at once he heard a steady breathing. Because he was so preoccupied with his wife, he thought he must be deceiving himself that he could hear her. He went over to the bed and found her lying there. He almost fainted with joy, and but for the reassurance her breathing brought, he would certainly have died there on the spot.

I was too amazed to speak. On the previous evening, I had told him distinctly that I was going back home, that I would not be staying at the Greifenbachs' tonight; so why on earth had he come here? And I was all the more surprised that he had left his wife alone on this moonlit night, after the moon had already shown him her power.

Said Gamzu, "You are surprised that I have left Gemulah alone?"

"Yes, I certainly am surprised."

Gamzu smiled with his live eye, or perhaps with his dead eye, and said, "Even if Gemulah wakes up now, even if she gets out of bed, she will not go walking."

"Have you found the talisman?" I asked.

"No, I haven't."

"If so, how do you come to leave your wife alone? Did the moon give you its personal guarantee that it would let your wife sleep in peace tonight? Seriously, Reb Gabriel, what makes you so confident?"

"I have found a cure."

"You consulted the doctors, did you, and got a prescription?"

"I did not consult the doctors," said Gamzu. "I am not in the habit of going to doctors, for even if they know the names of all the diseases there are and the names of all the drugs for them, I do not rely on their kind. I put my reliance on one who has drawn his strength from the Torah, for he knows and can find a cure for every part of the body, and needless to say, I rely on him in matters that affect the soul."

"And have you found such a man, and has he provided a cure for Gemulah?"

"The cure was already at hand. When I was studying at the yeshiva of Rabbi Shmuel Rosenberg at Innsdorf, a woman came to the rabbi and told him that a certain youth was lodging in her house, who was sick in mind and moonstruck, so that every month at the new moon he would go through the window and climb along the roofs, endangering himself, for if he were to wake up in the course of his walking it was to be feared that he might fall and be killed. They had already consulted doctors and no remedy had been found. Rabbi Shmuel said to her, 'Take a thick garment, and steep it in cold water until it is well soaked, and leave the garment beside the young man's bed. When he has climbed out of bed and his feet touch the cold garment, the chill will wake him at once and he will get back into bed again.' She did this and he was cured. Tonight I too did this, and I am sure that even if Gemulah should wake and stand up, she would immediately go back to bed."

I sat there, still puzzled. If this was the cure, why hadn't Gamzu made use of it before? Gamzu sensed what I was thinking and said, "You are surprised that I have waited until now."

"I am not surprised. With all your great devotion to charms that are above nature, you paid no attention to the remedies that are in nature itself."

"I can give you two answers. One is that the charms you speak of are also in general to be thought of as medicines. Once, for example, I took sick while I was on a journey, and was cured by means of charms. And when I went to Europe and told the specialists, they said, 'The charms you used are known drugs, which used to be employed in treatment until better and more convenient drugs were found.' As for my waiting until now, heaven caused me to forget the remedy of the great rabbi as a token of respect for him, because I gave up attending his yeshiva and went on to others. And as for my remembering today, it was because the object was at hand. I happened to be mending a tear in my clothes, and as I sat holding the garment I remembered the whole affair. I got up at once and put the article into water, and when it was soaked I spread it out before Gemulah's bed."

"Now," I said, "I am going to ask you a simple question. Was it because you did not find me at home that you came here?"

"I did not go to your home and I did not think of coming here."

"And yet you came."

"I came," said Gamzu, "but not intentionally."

"You see, Reb Gabriel, your heart is truer than your conscious mind, and it sent you here so that you would keep your promise to let me know how your wife is."

"The fact of the matter is this," said Gamzu; "I was at home watching Gemulah as she slept. I thought to myself, Now that Gemulah is asleep I shall go and pay a call on Amrami. I tested the garment I had left by her bed, soaked it in water again, and went out. As I walked, I reflected on Amrami. He was born in Jerusalem and grew up here. After spending forty or fifty years out of the country, he came back home, with nothing left of all he had acquired in those forty or fifty years, except for a little granddaughter and a few Hebrew books. Thinking of this I began to consider all those others raised in the Land of Israel who had left the country at about that time, rejecting the Land for the sake of a comfortable living abroad. Some of them were successful; some of them grew wealthy. Then came the Great Persecution, which took from them all they had, and back they came again to the Land of Israel. Now they complain and grumble that the country has become estranged from them. While I was thinking of how they complain, and while I gave no thought to their sufferings, I suddenly heard someone screaming. I went in the direction of the noise and saw a girl calling out to a young man: 'Günther, my darling! You're still alive, my darling! The Arab didn't wound you!' What was it all about? A young fellow and a girl were taking a walk in one of the valleys on the outskirts of the city. An Arab came up and began to annoy them. The young man shouted at him to chase him off. The Arab pulled out a knife and threatened the youth. The girl was in a panic because she thought he had been stabbed. In the meantime, I had gone out of my way and found myself down in the valley. I stood and wondered, Why am I here? I had meant to go to Amrami's, and instead, I have come to this house. Can you understand this? I cannot, just as yesterday I could not understand what had brought me here."

I answered, "Have not the rabbis said, 'To the place where a man is summoned, there his feet carry him?' But a man does not always know to what end he is summoned."

"So it is," said Gamzu. "To the place where a man is summoned his feet carry him. Whether he wishes it or not, his feet carry him there. Many have asked me how the hymns of Rabbi Adiel came into my possession. You too have asked me, if not in so many words, most certainly in your thoughts."

"Whether I have asked you or not, you have still not told me how it came about."

"If you wish, I shall tell you."

"If that is your wish, proceed."

Said Gamzu: "I came once to a certain village, and my feet would not allow me to go on from there. I said to myself, Nothing could be so patently foolish as to waste time in this wretched place, where the Jews have little knowledge of the Torah and are stricken with poverty. They can scarcely support themselves by their work on the soil and by the fruit which they buy from the Gentiles straight off the tree and sell to the dealers in the city. Do you expect to find books among men like these? In the meantime the Sabbath began. I found a bed at the house of a man who packed dried figs and dates, and went with him to the synagogue, a structure of palm-wood blackened with age. All the congregation assembled. They took off their shoes and kindled the earthenware lamp; they seated themselves and recited the Song of Songs; they stood and recited the Sabbath psalm and read the daily prayer 'And He is merciful' as on weekdays. And the prayers for the Sabbath were sung to their own melodies with which none of us is familiar, but which make their appeal to everyone who has a Jewish heart in his breast. So it was with their customs, which were handed down by their fathers, who had received them from their forefathers, as far back as the exiles of Jerusalem who were expelled by Nebuchadnezzar, king of Babylon. When he exiled Israel from Jerusalem, he ordered all the millstones in the land of Israel to be removed and loaded on to the shoulders of the young men. The young men went into exile laden with the millstones, and of them Jeremiah said, 'The young men carried a grinding mill,' and it is said,

'He weakened my strength on the way.' But the Presence saw their grief and poured life into the very stones, so that they mounted on high like wings and carried the young men away to a place where there was no oppressor. There the young men set down the millstones, and laid them as foundations for their synagogues, and from those that were left they built the foundations for their homes. And among these young men were some with a great knowledge of the Torah, who were learned in its mysteries and filled with the holy spirit. Many times have I pondered to myself whether their customs were not more pleasing to the Omnipresent than ours. So they set down the stones, and laid them as a foundation for the synagogues, and established a great settlement, virtually a kingdom. But still there was cause for anxiety, lest, heaven forbid, they should perish from the earth, for they had no wives. Then God gave light to their eyes, and they saw maidens coming up from the sea, of whom it is written, 'From Bashan I shall bring them back, I shall bring them from the depths of the sea.' Each man took himself a wife from among them, and they bore sons and daughters, and passed their days and years in delight. So things continued for several generations, until in their abundance of good they forgot Jerusalem. And when Ezra wrote to them, 'Go up to Jerusalem,' they did not go, for they said the Presence had given them this place instead of Jerusalem. Then there came against them the armed troops of the Gentiles, and went to war with them, and made great destruction among them, and few remained where once there had been many. Those who were left alive turned completely penitent and remembered Jerusalem and recognized, too, that those Gentiles had come against them only that they might be duly punished. Now I shall return to what I began to tell you.

"After the service they went to greet each other with kisses on the shoulder and beard, and wished each other a peaceful Sabbath and left for their homes after this exchange of Sabbath blessings. I went back with my host and dined with him, his two wives and his children all seated on the mat as they ate and drank and sang hymns which were unfamiliar to me and which I had not come across in any collection. Before sunrise I awoke to the sound of singing, and saw the master of the house seated on his mat as he raised his voice in hymns of praise. I duly washed my hands and listened attentively to these poems which I had never heard in my life, never seen in any book of devotional verse. So moved was I by their sweetness and holiness that it did not occur to me to inquire who was their author nor how they had reached this simple villager. But even had I asked, he would have declined to answer, for in those parts they avoid speaking before they have said their prayers. After he had finished his hymn-singing, we went to the synagogue, their custom being to pray at dawn.

"The entire community was gathered in the synagogue, seated round the four walls, singing psalms. Their way is for one of the congregation to recite a single psalm in a loud voice, word by word; after him, another takes his place, and then another. It is as if each man is given an audition to discover if he is fit to be an emissary of Israel before the Divine Presence; after finishing the psalm he lowers his voice, realizing that he is not fit for such a mission. When they reached the blessing for the daily renewal of light, the leader of the congregation came down from the dais and stood before the Ark, where he recited the call to prayer and the blessing for light, and then returned to his place.

The congregation went on with the regular order of the Service through to the end of the Silent Devotion. For the repetition of the prayer, the leader again took his place before the Ark, while the congregation stood with willing heart, and responded 'Amen' with great devotion. While taking the Torah scroll from the Ark, their way is to say 'Happy is the people whose lot is thus' and 'The Lord will reign.' And their scrolls are of deerskin, the writing is in large letters, and they do not allow more than the prescribed seven readers of the weekly portion. To the reading of the Torah the women come, and sit down in the synagogue on each side of the door; and I heard that this was an ancient custom which not even the most righteous or saintly of men had ever opposed. For at the time when the Torah was given to Israel, no evil desire could prevail; and to this day it cannot prevail with those whose thoughts are wholly upon the Torah.

"After the prayers I went home with my host. He seated himself on his mat and began with melodious hymns to the Divine Presence, who had chosen His people Israel and given them the Sabbath day.

Next he sang in praise of Israel, the people who had been so honored; and then in praise of the Sabbath, which, being holy, makes all who keep it holy. Afterwards we washed our hands and ate the chief meal of the day. The meal ended, but not the singing of hymns. I asked him about these hymns, about their origin. He said, 'I have them from my father. He was a great scholar and knew all that is in the books.' 'And where do the books come from?' He reached into a recess in the wall and brought out a bundle of writings, containing a great number of awe-inspiring devotional poems. Some were by Rabbi Dosa the son of Rabbi Penuel who originated the hymn *El Adon* and in his great humility did not sign his name to it, except in the fourth line, where he wrote of how the two great angels Knowledge and Understanding, who encircle the majesty of the Holy One, revealed themselves to him; and as he wrote of their works he introduced his name in an acrostic. In similar fashion I identified the poems of Rabbi Adiel, who composed the hymn, 'This people which Thou didst create, Thy holy commandments they shall keep,' and similarly those of other early poets who concealed their names. I broached the question of his selling me his book. He said, 'Even if you gave me an ox I would not sell it.' I asked him for permission to copy two or three of the poems. He said, 'Even if you gave me a sheep I would not let you.' He would not sell his book even in return for an ox, nor let me make copies even for a sheep. I went away despairing and came back to the city. Three days later he came to my home and presented the volume to me as a gift. I offered to pay him what it was worth; he would not agree. I raised the sum, and still he refused. I said, 'Even that amount, it seems, is not equal to the value you set upon it.' He answered, 'God forbid that I should take it. I am giving the book to you for nothing.' 'But why?' I asked. 'What concern is that of yours?' he said. 'You want it, and I am giving it to you.' I said, 'I do not wish to take it without payment. I shall give you what it is worth.' He put his hands behind his back and went away. It was hard for me to take a precious article like this from a poor man. I went to the learned men of the city to seek their advice; as soon as they saw me coming they hastened to meet me and greeted me with great deference. I said, 'My masters, why have you seen fit to do me such honor?' 'How else could it be,' they said, 'seeing that you are favored by heaven?' 'I do not deserve to be addressed in this way,' I said. 'Why do you think that I am favored on high?' They answered, 'There came a villager, who told us that he was instructed in a dream to give you a holy volume in manuscript which he had inherited from his father, who had it from his father, and so back for many generations.' I said, 'I have come to you because of this book. Set a value upon it and I shall leave the money with you.' They answered: 'God forbid that we should take money from you.' I said, 'I swear that I will not budge from here until you tell me how much I must pay.' When they saw that I was determined, they agreed to take from me a certain sum of gold dinars, and I left the sum with them. I do not know if the poor villager took what I left for him or not. Possibly he was told in his dream to give the money to charity, and did so. That is the story of the collection of devotional poems which came into my possession not long before I became acquainted with Gemulah."

VI

Perfect as the moon was Gemulah; her eyes were sparks of light; her face was like the morning star; her voice was sweet as the shades of evening. When she lifted up her voice in song, it was as if all the gates of melody were opened. She knew, besides, how to bake *kavanim* and how to roast meat on hot coals. Though Gemulah was only twelve years old when Gamzu first chanced upon her home, her wisdom shone out like that of a mature woman, for her father had passed on to her the secret knowledge laid up by his ancestors. She was his only child, his wife having died in giving birth to her. He had taken no other wife, and since he could not bear to think of so much wisdom perishing, he had handed on what he knew to his daughter.

Gamzu spent about a year in her father's house, until his strength began to return to him. Then he went his way and traveled to Vienna to have his eye treated. He spent a year in Vienna and left with one eye only. All the time he was in the hospital he consoled himself with the thought that his sight would return and he would then go back to Gemulah. When he left the hospital he had no funds for travel; all his resources had been eaten up in doctors' fees. Akiva

Amrami met him and said, "Obadiah and Obadiowitz are seeking a man like you, who would be willing to travel on their behalf to distant countries and bring back rare books." He went to see Obadiah and Obadiowitz; they marked out all the places he was to go to, paid his traveling expenses, and authorized him to spend on their account as much as he needed. God prospered his way and Gamzu gave satisfaction to his employers. He was able to save some of his earnings, and so he set out for the land where Gemulah lived.

In the meantime something had happened in Gemulah's country, the like of which hardly occurred once in a jubilee cycle. A holy man, a *Hakham* of Jerusalem, had appeared there and stayed for six months. Six more months had already gone by since his departure, yet his name was still on everybody's lips. Those who had been sick spoke of how *Hakham* Gideon had relieved their suffering. Others told of how *Hakham* Gideon had taught them ways to ease the burdens of life. He had also shown how all kinds of illnesses might be avoided, even without incantations, even in the case of infants who normally die of the evil eye. He had taken no fees from them, and if they had given him a present he had made them a gift in return. Gamzu was of the opinion that this *Hakham* Gideon was no Jerusalem *Hakham*, but a European man of learning, an ethnologist or something of the kind. He saw as evidence of this the fact that Gideon had recorded in his notebook all the songs he had heard from Gemulah and even her conversations with her father in the language they had devised for themselves.

So Gamzu returned to Gemulah's home, and when Gemulah saw him, she rejoiced as a bride over her bridegroom. She roasted a kid for him and baked *kavanim* and sang for him all the songs that *Hakham* Gideon had liked. Nor did she concern herself with the affairs of Gadi Ben Ge'im, her neighbor, who insisted that Gemulah had been betrothed to him since the time when they were nursed together at his mother's breast; for Gemulah's mother having died in giving birth to her, the mother of Gadi had reared her as a daughter.

At this time evil fell upon Gevariah, Gemulah's father. He had gone up to the mountaintop to learn from the eagles how they renew their youth. There an eagle had attacked him, not heeding the fact that Gevariah came in peace, without any weapon, not even a stick. Gevariah fought back, and had he not managed to beat off the eagle, he would have been mauled beneath its talons and torn to pieces and devoured. Even so, the eagle injured his left arm, lacerating the flesh. Gevariah neglected the wound until he took sick and died.

Before his death, he appointed a night of dancing, for his own and Gemulah's sake, for such was the custom in their country. Seven nights before a betrothal they appoint a night of dances, and it is usual on such occasions for the young men to come, and each snatches a wife for himself from among the girl dancers. Gamzu was aware that Gadi Ben Ge'im intended to snatch Gemulah, but he anticipated him and won her and made her his bride.

For seven days and seven nights they held the wedding feast. Gevariah lay upon his mat and conducted the dances with his uninjured hand. Seven different dances he conducted each night, and eight kinds of dances each day, that Gemulah might give birth to a son who would be circumcised on the eighth day. With the end of the seven days of feasting, Gevariah's life ended, too.

Gemulah mourned her father for seven days and nights, with songs of lamentation every day and night. At the end of her first week of mourning she made a great memorial, with songs and dances full of dread and wonder. After thirty days had passed, Gamzu began to speak to her of the journey they must take. Gemulah heard him out, but could not grasp what this meant for her. When she understood she protested strongly. Little by little she was persuaded, until she consented to leave, but she put off making the journey from week to week and from month to month. All this time the moon did not affect her; it seemed that because of her grief at her father's death the moon had no power over her. She was also protected by the charms, though there was no change in her condition, and she was like an unripe fig that is still closed up, on the tree, her sweetness all stored within. At the end of the year of mourning, she said of her own accord that she was ready for the journey. Gamzu hired two camels, and they rode until they came to the edge of the desert, where the caravans go out. They joined a caravan, journeying for forty days until they came to a settled region. Gamzu bought shoes for her feet

and dresses for her to wear and a kerchief for her head, and they rode
on until they reached a port. There he hired a ship, and they sailed
to the Land of Israel. And because they were traveling to the Land
of Israel, God preserved them from all evil. But it was not so in the
Land itself. As Rabbi Alshikh wrote, concerning the dispute in the
Talmud as to whether a man is judged every day or on Rosh Hashanah only: the latter applies outside the Land, but in the Land of Israel
one is judged daily; each single day the Holy One sits in judgment
upon His people. The beginning of the judgment was that Gemulah
no longer sang her sweet songs. Later, all speech was withheld from
her. Next, she was possessed by melancholy. Lastly, she fell seriously
ill. With her sickness she began to torment Gamzu. His plight grew
worse from day to day.

As Gamzu was relating this, I heard a sound like the opening of a window. At the same moment I could hear spoken words.
I was not afraid, but I was certainly astonished, since besides myself
and Gamzu there was no one in the house, and neither he nor I had
opened a window. I began to recollect the dream I had had on the
previous night, the train I saw and the window that opened. And
again I was amazed at the power of dreams, which come back to us
when we are awake as if they were real happenings. Once more I heard
the same sound. I listened attentively and thought, Ginat must have
come home and opened a window. But how could one explain the
sound of spoken words? Gamzu saw I was distracted, and said, "You
are tired. Do you want to sleep?"

"No, I am not tired, and I don't want to sleep."

"Are you troubled about something?"

"I can hear footsteps."

"If I can trust my own ears," said Gamzu, "there has not been
a sound or even an echo of one."

"If that is so, I must be mistaken. Let us go back to what we
were talking about."

Gamzu began to speak again about his experiences with Gemulah in Jerusalem. Many a time her life had hung by a thread, and
had not the Holy One helped him, he would not have been able to
endure his distress for a single day. But God's mercies are great. He

sends a man afflictions, but He also gives him the strength to withstand them.

I do not remember the exact sequence of Gamzu's remarks, but I recall that he told me again about the garment, and in bringing this to mind made mention of his teacher. Having spoken of him, he also mentioned the time of his youth, which he had spent as a student in yeshivas.

You know Gamzu as a man with many connections, in demand among scholars of the East and West alike for books and manuscripts. But he had begun as any other yeshiva student, boarding out on the charity of the local townspeople. Once a certain householder sent him to buy a copy of the *Concise Shulhan Arukh*. At the bookseller's he came across a book quite different from the rest. Every other line of print was indented, and every word had vowel points; some lines resembled the Great Hymn of Praise sung by the ministering angels, some the confessional *Al Het*. He looked at it for a long while, full of wonder; never in his life had he seen a book like this. The bookseller watched him, and told him he could have it for forty kreutzer. For a yeshiva student, forty kreutzer was a large sum; even if he sold his long coat, he would not get that amount for it. But he had a box which a carpenter had made him in return for giving lessons to his son. It was something of a luxury, since all his possessions, apart from the clothes which he stood up in, could be wrapped in his shirt; but it gave him the kind of pleasure one feels in owning an article of intrinsic beauty. He gave his box to the bookseller and received the book. It was the *divan* of the poems of Judah Halevi, edited by S. D. Luzzatto. He read it again and again, until he knew all the poems by heart. And still he was unsatisfied. He began to pore over festival prayers and penitential hymns and elegies and old prayer books, reading and transcribing for himself. He could not afford the paper to copy down all the things he liked, so he noted down only the opening lines as reminders. Because he was so fastened to poetry, he came unfastened at the yeshiva. Accordingly he went and hired himself out to a bookseller. The shopkeeper could see that he knew a great deal, and sent him out to widows with the books of their husbands left on their hands, as well as to the "enlightened" rich who were clearing their homes of sacred literature. In time he began to make his own purchases. Later, he started traveling to far-off countries, and still later, to lands which no European had ever crossed. He reached the farthest edge of the desert and brought out books and manuscripts of which the most eminent bibliographers had no knowledge, as well as *divans* by anonymous poets who in their holiness and humility had left no record of their names.

Gamzu rolled himself a cigarette and laid it down. He rubbed his dead eye, smiled out of his good eye, and again took up the cigarette, holding it unlit between his fingers and saying, "When I pass over to the next world, they will lead me to the place where carcasses like me belong. I shall lie there in my shame, justifying the divine decree that I have been left exactly where I am, telling myself I have no right to expect anything better, naked as I am of merit and good works. At that moment, rank upon rank of demons will be massing against me, created out of my own sins. They will rise on high before the seat of judgment to accuse me and make hell deep for me. While waiting for the sentence, what shall I do? I shall recite from memory the hymns I know, until I forget where I am, and become so excited by them that I shall start shouting them aloud. The holy poets will hear me and say, 'What noise is that from the grave? Let us go and see.' They will come down and see this wretched soul and take me up in their hallowed hands, saying, 'You are the man who rescued us from the depths of oblivion.' And they will smile at me in the humility of their virtue and say, 'Gabriel Gamzu, come with us.' So they will bring me to dwell with them, and I will find shelter in the shade of their holiness. That is how I console myself in my misery."

Gamzu sat there smiling, with the expression of a man who knowingly deceives himself and is aware that he is only joking at his own expense. But I knew him very well; I understood that he believed in what he had said, more completely, perhaps, than he would admit to himself. I looked at his face, the face of a Jew out of the Middle Ages, reincarnated in this generation in order to procure manuscripts and early prints for scholars and investigators, enabling them to write observations and annotations and bibliographies, so that men like me might read these works and delight in the beauty of their verse.

Thus Gamzu bore his sufferings and solaced himself with the thought of better things to come. Meanwhile he was fully taken up with the troubles of his wife, an incurable invalid. I began to speak to him about nursing homes where the sick receive some degree of attention. "It would be a good idea to place Gemulah in a nursing home," I said. "As for the cost, I have here the first payment of twelve pounds; the rest will surely come."

Gamzu blew on his skullcap. "Those twelve pounds," he said, "are what I received for the manuscripts I sold to whoever got the talismans." I asked if he suspected this person of taking the magic objects by deceit.

"I am not a suspicious man," he said. "It is possible that whoever took them did not notice them at first, and when he did so, told himself that since they had come into his possession they were his. Or perhaps he believed that the charms were part of the lot he had bought. He may sometimes have thought one way, and sometimes another. Morality admits of compromise, and a man can still be moral even if he compromises according to his need; especially where books are concerned."

"Do you suppose," I asked, "that he knows the properties of the charms?"

"How should he know? If an article of that kind came into my hands by chance, and no one told me what it was, would *I* know? Besides, all these scholars are modern men; even if you were to reveal the properties of the charms, they would only laugh at you; and if they bought them, it would be as specimens of folklore. Ah, folklore, folklore! Everything which is not material for scientific research they treat as folklore. Have they not made our holy Torah into either one or the other? People live out their lives according to the Torah, they lay down their lives for the heritage of their fathers; then along come the scholars, and make the Torah into 'research material,' and the ways of our fathers into folklore."

I listened carefully to what Gamzu said, and thought of those scholars who acquire what their original owners regarded as articles of magic, but which for those who have bought them are only so much bric-a-brac; and I thought, too, of this poor Gamzu, afflicted and dejected, whom the Holy One had crushed with sorrow. If we are allowed to judge a man by his deeds, surely it was not for the deeds Gamzu had done in this incarnation that he had been so doomed. But who was I to involve myself in these issues? Such as I was, I should be satisfied that the Holy One had, in a manner of speaking, not looked in my direction for some little while. I passed my hand over my forehead as if to set these thoughts aside, and gave all my attention to my companion.

There he sat, in a strange posture, his head bent to one side and an ear turned towards the wall. After a considerable lapse of time, in which he still kept his ear averted, I said, "You look as if you can hear what the stones in the walls are saying to one another."

He stared at me without reply and went on listening, his ear concentrated on the wall and both eyes aflame. There was no difference between his good eye and his dead eye, except that one was full of amazement and the other grew more and more irate. I took it that he was listening to matters which made him angry, and asked, "Can you hear anything?"

He stirred as though from sleep. "I can hear nothing, nothing at all. And what about you? Do you hear anything?"

"No, nothing," I answered.

He rubbed his ear. "Well then, it must be a hallucination."

He began to feel about in his pockets, produced some tobacco, and set it down. Then he extracted a handkerchief and laid that down, too. Next he stroked with his fingers the space between his nose and beard, then passed his hand over his beard, and finally said, "Didn't you say you could hear footsteps?"

"When did I say that?"

"When? Just a little while ago you said it."

"And didn't you answer that there was not a sound, nor the slightest suspicion of a sound?"

"So I said," he replied, "and so I am still inclined to think. But if you were to tell me now that you can hear something, I should not contradict you."

"Then you did hear something?"

"No, I didn't," he answered.

"Very well," I said, "let's return to our previous subject. What were we talking about before?"

"I swear, I don't remember."

"Does what you say count so little to you," I asked, "that you don't even try to remember it?"

"On the contrary."

"Why 'on the contrary'?"

"Because talk between two men of Israel is important, just as songs and hymns are; when you try to repeat them, the tune is never the same. Listen, I have just had an idea. I shall take Gemulah to the village of Atruz."

"To Atruz? Why?"

"Atruz is the name for Atrot Gad, which is in the territory of Gad, and Gemulah is of the tribe of Gad. She will breathe the odor of her own land and recover her health. I shall never forget how glad she was of my presence when Gadi Ben Ge'im was about to snatch her and I anticipated him and seized her first. I would give the whole world only to hear Gemulah laugh again as she laughed at that moment. But now let me ask you about that doctor, not Dr. Greifenbach, but Dr. Ginat. Everything you have told me about him pleases me. Our sages of blessed memory have said, 'Who is wise? He who knows his place.' If it were not wrong to add to their words, I should continue, 'when others do not know it.' At any rate, I am surprised that you live with him in the same house and have not come to know him. Is he old or young? How do you like his books? You have made me curious about matters I have not given any thought to. Why is this?"

I said, "See how many of our savants have been given high positions, and the journalists hang on to what they say and make them into worldwide celebrities, yet we ignore them. But this great scholar has no post, no articles are written in his praise; yet we wonder at him and try to know more about him. Even you, Mr. Gamzu, have undertaken to read his books in your second or third incarnation, and already in this one he arouses your curiosity."

Suddenly the colors began to change in Gamzu's face, until at last all color left it, and there remained only a pale cast that gradually darkened, leaving his features like formless clay. Within that clay without form, I read a kind of horrified amazement. Contemplating it, I was so shocked that my hair stood on end, for never in my life had I seen a living man so completely divest himself of his own likeness. Gamzu took hold of my hand and said, "What's the matter?"

I sat speechless. When I withdrew my hand from his, he did not even notice. "What happened to you?" I asked.

Roused from his trance, he smiled in an embarrassed fashion, waved his hand and said, "Idiot that I am, I've been fooled by my senses."

"What is your answer, then?" I asked.

"I don't know what you are referring to," he replied.

"To the suggestion of the nursing home."

He waved his hand again. "My mind is not on that now."

"And when will you put your mind to it?"

"Not now, at any rate."

I began to describe to Gamzu how much he would benefit if he sent his wife to the nursing home. "It would certainly be good for Gemulah to be there, and you too, Mr. Gamzu, would take new heart; then perhaps you would go on your travels again and discover new hidden treasures. These days, it is as if the earth had opened up and brought forth all that the first ages of man stored away. Has not Ginat discovered things that were concealed for thousands of years, the Edo language and the Enamite Hymns? But why should I mention Ginat? Haven't you yourself discovered ancient treasures that were unknown to us?"

Gamzu looked at me, but his ears were inclined elsewhere. Sometimes he turned them in the direction of the door, sometimes toward the window, and betweentimes toward the wall. I was irritated with him. "What a brain you have, Reb Gabriel. It is not enough that you listen simultaneously to what the door, the window and the wall are saying to one another; you even take note of every word spoken by a mere man like me."

Gamzu stared at me. "What did you say?"

"I didn't say anything," I replied.

"I was convinced that I heard people speaking."

In my annoyance I answered, "If so, tell me in what language they spoke. Was it in Edo, or Enam?"

Gamzu realized that I was angry. In a broken voice he said, "Believe it or not, they spoke that very language."

"What language?"

"The language that Gemulah used to speak to her father, the language they made up to amuse themselves. My nerves are in such a state that I believe I hear things impossible to hear; and I am not far from saying that what I hear sounds like Gemulah's voice."

I sat quiet, making no reply; for what indeed should I say to a man whose spirit has been broken by his troubles and who seeks to console himself with that which gave him pleasure in the days when he enjoyed peace of mind? Gamzu's blood had drained away from his face; only his ears seemed to be alive. He sat there and hearkened with those ears which were all that was left to him of his whole motionless being. In the end he waved his hand in dismissal and said, "It is all mere fancy." He smiled with embarrassment, adding, "When a man's imagination gets the better of him, the merest shadow of a wall seems like a substantial thing. What is the time? It is time for me to go back home. I am worried that the garment I put down before Gemulah's bed may have dried up by now. In the Land of Israel even the moon gives off more heat than the sun in other countries."

He stood up, then sat down again. Seated, he stared straight ahead and muttered sorrowfully to himself, "And a word was secretly brought to me, and mine ear received a whisper thereof."

"You are sad," I said.

He smiled. "It is not I who am sad. Those words were spoken by Job. He was the sad one."

I surveyed him and tried to think of what I could say. I felt in my pocket, like a man who has been searching in the recesses of his heart and ends by rummaging through his possessions. In so doing I brought out a picture postcard that had reached me from Greifenbach and his wife. I looked at it and saw depicted there a kind of moon shape resting on a roof. Gamzu took out some paper and tobacco, and rolled himself a cigarette. He licked the edges of the paper and put the cigarette between his lips and lit it. "Won't you smoke?" he asked. "Let me roll you a cigarette."

"Don't trouble, friend," I said, and taking out a pack of cigarettes, I lit one for myself.

We sat smoking together; the smoke of the cigarettes rose in the air, and our conversation came to a halt. I looked at the smoke and began to reflect in silence. If Gamzu gets up to leave, I said to myself, I shall not tell him to sit down again; and if he goes, I shall not call him back. When he has left, I shall make my bed and lie down. And God willing, tomorrow I shall write a letter to Gerhard and Gerda saying, "Your house is being well looked after." As for my own home, I am not worried, for after the thieves broke in I had strong new locks made.

Now my thoughts turned to my wife and children, who were staying in the country. Away from the city, they would certainly be asleep by now, for village people go to bed early. I too should be asleep were it not for Gamzu. As for Gamzu, wasn't it strange that he had come here? What would he have done if he had not found me? I reached out and tilted the lamp over to the other side. The moon came and shone straight into the room. My eyelids closed involuntarily, my head began to nod. With an effort I looked up to see if Gamzu had noticed that I was falling asleep. I saw that his fist was clenched and laid against his lips. Saying nothing, I thought: Why should he have put his hand over his lips? If he wants to hint that I am not to speak, I am not speaking anyhow. From so much thinking my head grew heavy; my eyelids were heavy too. My head sank down on my breast; the lids closed over my eyes.

Both my eyes were closed, craving a little sleep. But my ears were not ready for sleep, because of the sound of bare feet on the stone floor of the nearby room. I bent my ear and heard a voice singing, *"Yiddal, yiddal, yiddal, vah, pah, mah; yid-dal, yiddal, yiddal, vah, pah, mah."* I am back in my dream again, I thought. The moon shone straight upon my eyes. I said to the moon, "I know you. You are the one, aren't you, whose face was on the picture postcard." Again the voice sang, *"Yiddal, yiddal, yiddal, vah, pah, mah."* The moon lit up the voice, and within the voice was the likeness of a woman. If that is so, I said to myself, then Greifenbach spoke the truth when he said that Ginat had created a girl for himself. But this pain in my fingers, where has it come from all of a sudden?

I opened my eyes and saw Gamzu standing beside me pressing my hand. Taking my hand out of his, I looked at him in amazement. Gamzu sat down again. He closed his live eye and let it set in sleep, but his dead eye began to burn. Why did he squeeze my fingers, I wondered. Because he wanted me to listen to the song. So there really was a song, a song in waking and not only in dream. What song, then? It was a woman's, and she was beating time with her feet. I laughed inwardly at my having been ready to think of her as a girl created by the imagination. And to rid myself of all doubt, I made up my mind to ask Gamzu what he thought. Gamzu had closed his dead eye together with his live eye, and his face wore a smile of delight, like that of a young man who hears his true love speaking. It was hard to break in upon his rapture. I lowered my eyes and sat in silence.

There was the sound again, no longer the sound of singing now, but of spoken words. In what language? In a tongue that was unlike those we know. I wanted to ask Gamzu about it. I opened my eyes and saw that his chair was vacant. I looked all around but could not see him. I stood up and went from room to room without finding him, and came back and sat down again. About ten minutes passed, but he did not return. I began to feel anxious lest something had happened to him. Getting up from my chair, I went out into the hall. Gamzu was not to be found. I shall wait for him in my room, I thought. Before I could manage to return, I entered a room which had been built as a *sukkah* for the festival and was now serving as an anteroom to that of Ginat. I looked around me, and saw Gamzu standing behind the door; I wondered what on earth he was doing there. The palm of a hand reached out and touched the door. Before I could decide whether what I saw was really seen or not, the door opened half way and the light in the room shone out brightly. It drew me and I looked inside.

Moonlight filled the room, and in the room stood a young woman wrapped in white, her feet bare, her hair disheveled, her eyes closed. And a young man sat at the table by the window and wrote in ink on paper all that she spoke. I did not comprehend one word of her speech, and I doubt if there is any man in the world who could understand a language mysterious as this. Still the woman spoke and the pen wrote. And this was clear, that the man writing down the woman's words was Ginat. When had he returned, when had he gone to his room? He must have come back while Gamzu and I were sitting in Greifenbach's room, and the woman must have gotten in through the window. That was why I had heard a window being opened and the sound of bare feet. With all the things I was seeing in quick succession I forgot Gamzu, and did not notice that he was standing beside me. But then Gamzu—yes, Gamzu!—did a strange thing. He forgot all manners and proprieties. He flung himself into the room and twined his arms around the woman's waist. This chaste man, who had devoted his entire being to his wife, burst into a strange room and embraced a strange woman.

And now things began to get confused, and I am surprised that I can remember their sequence. These events all happened in a short time, yet how long it seemed. I stood with Gamzu facing the room of Ginat, and the door was half open. I peeped into the room, which was lit up by the moon. The moon had shrunk in order to get inside, but once in, she proceeded to expand until the whole room and its contents were visible. I saw a woman standing there, and a young man seated before the table writing. Gamzu suddenly rushed in and clasped the woman's waist with his arms. The woman drew back her head from him, and still in his embrace, cried out, "*Hakham!*" Her voice was that of a maiden whose love has fully ripened.

The young man answered, "Go, Gemulah, follow your husband."

Gemulah said, "After all the years that I have waited for you! Now you say, 'Go, Gemulah.'"

"He is your husband," the young man said.

"And you, *Hakham* Gideon," said Gemulah, "what are you to me?"

"I am nothing."

Gemulah laughed. "So you are nothing! You are a good man, you are a lovely man, in all the world there is no man so good and so lovely as you. Let me stay with you, and I shall sing you the song of the bird Grofit, which she sings only once in her lifetime."

"Sing," said the young man.

Gemulah said, "I shall sing the song of Grofit, and then we shall die. Gabriel, when *Hakham* Gideon and I are dead, dig us two graves side by side. Do you promise you will do that?"

Gamzu put his hand over her mouth and held on with all his might. She struggled to escape from his arms, but he held her tight and shouted to Ginat, "Do you know what you are? A sinner in Israel, that's what you are! You are not even afraid to steal another man's wife!"

"Don't listen to him, *Hakham* Gideon," cried Gemulah. "I am not any man's wife. Ask him, has he ever seen my naked body?"

Gamzu let out a long and bitter sigh. "You are my wife," he said, "my wife, my wife! You are consecrated to me by the law of Moses and of Israel."

The young man said, "Go, Gemulah, go with your husband."

"So you reject me," said Gemulah.

"I do not reject you, Gemulah," said the young man, "I only tell you what you must do."

With that, her strength left her, and were it not that Gamzu still held her she would have fallen. And once Gamzu had grasped her, he did not let go of her until he took her up in his arms and went away, while Ginat and I looked on.

VII

The moon went her way, completing her journey of thirty days. Thirty days had now passed since Gamzu took his wife back from the house of Ginat, and all this time I saw neither Ginat nor Gamzu. I did not see Gamzu because he did not come to my home, and I am not in the habit of going to his; as for Ginat, he went away immediately after that affair. I came across him once in an Arab coffeehouse, with Amram, the son of the Samaritan high priest. Since nothing came of it, I shall not dwell on it. Once again I found him in Giv'at Shaul, at the parchment workshop belonging to *Hakham* Gvilan and *Hakham* Gagin. Again, nothing came of it, and I shall not dwell on it.

My wife and children have returned from their holiday; the water has returned to the tanks, to the pipes, and to the taps. I stay at home and rarely go out, nor do I know how Gemulah has been faring with Gamzu since he took her back. Since, on balance, goodness outweighs evil, I assume that she has made her peace with him, and that having done so, her own language has returned to her. Perhaps she even allows herself to sing, and once more her voice stirs the heart like the voice of the bird Grofit; and as you know, Gamzu loves nothing so much as Gemulah's voice lifted in song. Why then did Gamzu lay his hand over her mouth to silence her? Because songs are conjoined, they are linked up one with another, the songs of the springs with the songs of high mountains, and those of high mountains with the songs of the birds of the air. And among these birds there is one whose name is Grofit; when its hour comes to leave the world, it looks up to the clouds and raises its voice in song; and when its song is ended, it departs from this world. All these songs are linked together in the language of Gemulah. Had she uttered that song of Grofit, her soul would have departed from her, and she would have died. For this reason Gamzu stopped up her mouth and preserved her soul that it might not depart.

I stay at home, then, and continue with my work, whether it be little or much. But when the sun sets I lay my work aside. "Behold that which I have seen: it is good, it is comely"—and so forth— "to toil under the sun," for so long as the sun shines upon the world, it is good, it is comely in the world. If I have a little strength left when my work is done, I go for a walk. Otherwise, I sit alone in front of my house or stand in the window and watch how the day passes and the night comes, how the stars take their places in the sky and the moon rises.

The moon and stars have not yet come out. But the sky gleams with its own light, burning from within, and a blue-grey glow, like the bloom on a ripe plum, hovers between heaven and earth, while the whole world is alive with the chirping of countless crickets. Not far from my house there is a commotion among the trees. It continues until it sounds like a forest on a stormy night, like a sea in tempest. I wonder if something is not astir in the world.

I have stood alone and looked behind the back of the world; and because so much has already happened, I have looked away from events that are at present taking shape. One of those past happenings was the affair of Gamzu and Gemulah: the story of a man who comes home and does not find his wife; going to the south, turning to the north, turning turning, he goes on, and at the last finds her in a house where he chances to be. But what truly amazed me was this: with my own eyes I had seen Gamzu snatch his wife away, and yet it seemed to me that it was only a story, like the one he himself had told me, of how on one occasion dances were held, and Gadi Ben Ge'im was about to seize Gemulah, and Gamzu forestalled him. There is no event whose mark has not gone before it. Such is the parable of the bird: before it flies, it spreads its wings and they make a shadow; it looks at the shadow, raises its wings, and flies away.

The moon has not yet appeared, but she is about to rise, and a place is set aside for her in the sky. Clouds that seemed a portion of the sky itself are parted now, moving this way and that on their course, while the moon ripens towards her rising. Happy is he who can make use of her light without being touched by it.

My thoughts turn to those who long for the moon. And from thoughts of the moon, to thoughts that are bound up and conjoined with the way earth binds us. And from earth to man. To those whom the earth welcomes, and those who wander about like the shades of night. I do not refer especially to that young couple who had not found a home for themselves; nor especially to those who left the country and, on their return, found that the land had become estranged from them. Nor do I mean in particular Greifenbach and his wife, who went abroad to take a rest from the strain of life in our country. I refer to all men who are in the grip of this earth.

Greifenbach and his wife are about to return. Their cleaning woman, Grazia, told me this; a picture postcard from Mrs. Greifenbach had come for her. I know this, too, from the contents of a card they wrote to me. And since they are about to arrive, I have been to see how their house is faring.

Their house is locked up. No one has broken in. I do not know if Ginat is in his room or not. At any rate, the window that opened for Gemulah is now closed. When the Greifenbachs return to Jerusalem, they will find everything securely in its place.

Next morning when I picked up the newspaper to see if the Greifenbachs' return was announced, I read that a Dr. Gilat was dead. Since I was not acquainted with any person of that name, I did not linger over the news. But my heart sank, and when a man's heart behaves irregularly, evil things begin to take shape. I began to wonder if there was a misprint and "l" had been substituted for "n." Once a man enters into evil speculations, they do not leave him. I took up the paper again and saw the letter "l" standing out plainly in the dead man's name, yet my eyes which could see the "l" also saw "n," as if the "l" had been twisted and turned into an "n." The matter troubled me so much that I got up and went out.

I looked at the announcements on the walls but found no declaration of his death. Ginat did not hold an official post and was not known in town; there was nobody to publicize his death on the billboards. But I learned from another source that he was indeed dead, and how his death came about.

I shall start at the beginning. I was walking the streets and reflecting to myself: If it was Ginat, why was the name written as Gilat? And if it was indeed Gilat, why do I have these forebodings?

Old Amrami, leaning upon his granddaughter, came across me and said, "Are you going to the funeral?"

I nodded and said that I was.

"What a strange case!" he said. "A woman who can't move from her bed meets her death on a roof."

I looked at him long and hard without knowing what he meant.

He went on to say, "Mysterious are the ways of God; who can understand them? A man risks his life to save another life in Israel, and the end of it is, he falls and is killed. So now we are not going to one funeral, but to two. To the funeral of Gamzu's wife, and to the funeral of Dr. Ginat."

Amrami's granddaughter Edna added, "The newspapers didn't report this, but eyewitnesses say that last night a gentleman went out of his room and saw a woman climbing up onto the roof. He rushed up to save her from danger, the parapet collapsed, and they both fell to their death."

So we walked, Amrami and Edna and I, until we reached the hospital where the bodies of Gemulah and Ginat had been brought. The hospital was closed. At the gate sat the porter, looking at passers-by, daydreaming that they were all asking his permission to go inside and were all being refused. But his luck was out; not a man asked if he might enter the hospital, but all went into the open courtyard where the mortuary stood.

At the side of the courtyard, standing apart, was the patients' laundry. Small as it was, it performed a service to the dead, for it fulfilled the obligation of hospitality by admitting visitors. Alongside it, on a broken bench, sat three members of the burial society, professional watchers of the dead, while a fourth stood up behind them and rolled himself a cigarette. He saw Amrami and me and attached himself to us, telling us that he had sat all night beside the corpse, reciting psalms for the dead. And who, he wanted to know, was going to pay him for saying those psalms? He could tell I was an honest man; he would grant me the *mitzvah* of paying him.

A family of mourners came and sat down on the bench opposite. A woman detached herself from the group and walked in front of them, raising her voice in loud wailing and laments, swaying her shrunken body to the rhythm. She was sad, very sad, and so was her voice. Not a word that she uttered could I understand, but her voice, her bearing, and the expression on her face moved all who saw her to tears. The woman took from her bosom the picture of a young man and gazed at it intently. Again she sang, in praise of his beauty and his grace, recounting all the years he would have had for life, had not the angel of death come for him too soon. All the mourners wept bitterly, and all who heard them wept in sympathy. Just so Gemulah must have wept for her father, just so she must have mourned him.

As I stood among them, I saw Gamzu coming out of the mortuary. The perplexity of soul that always accompanied him had left him for a while; in its place came two new companions, astonishment and sorrow. I went up to him and stood by his side. He rubbed his dead eye with his finger, then took out a handkerchief and wiped his finger, saying, "He was the one. He was the Jerusalem *Hakham*, and he was the scholar I sold the talismans to."

One of the mortuary attendants came over to us. He looked once at me and once at Gamzu, like a dealer who has two customers and wonders which he should attend to first. While trying to make up his mind which of us was the more important, he asked for a cigarette. Gamzu searched in his pocket and took out cigarette paper and tobacco. In the meantime they brought out Ginat's coffin. Gamzu lifted his finger to his dead eye and said calmly, "Ginat is the one who bought the talismans."

The coffin bearers moved on; about half the necessary Minyan, I and three or four others who were at hand, followed to perform the last rites. A beggar with a tin box approached. He banged on his box, calling repeatedly, "Charity saves from death." Each time he looked behind him, lest in the meanwhile other bodies had been brought out and he should stand to miss what the accompanying mourners might give him.

On the way back from the Mount of Olives, Gemulah's funeral procession caught up with me. And on the way back from Gemulah's funeral I was stopped by an automobile in which sat the Greifenbachs, just returned from their travels.

Greifenbach saw me and called from inside the automobile, "How nice to see you! How really nice! How is our house getting on? Is it still standing?"

Mrs. Greifenbach asked, "Has nobody broken in?"

"No," I answered, "no one has broken in."

Again she asked, "Did you get to know Ginat?"

"Yes," I said, "I got to know Ginat."

Both of them said together, "Get in and ride with us."

I answered, "Good, I shall get in and ride with you."

A policeman came along and shouted that we were holding up traffic. The driver started up the car, and the Greifenbachs went on without me.

Some days later, I went to the Greifenbachs to return their key. On the same day officials had come to examine Dr. Ginat's room, but they found nothing except his ordinary utensils and two tins full of the ash of burnt papers. The ash was probably made up of his writings. When had Ginat burnt these? On the night when Gamzu took

Gemulah back? Or on the same night that Ginat went out to save Gemulah and was killed with her?

What induced Ginat to destroy his own work, to burn in a few minutes the result of years of toil? As is usual in such cases, the question is disposed of lightly. It was psychological depression, they say; grave doubts brought him to this deed. But what led him to such a state of depression, and what were those doubts of his? To these questions no answer is forthcoming. For surely there is no way of estimating, no way of knowing or understanding such a matter, especially where one is dealing with an enlightened spirit such as Ginat, and with works of wisdom and poetry such as his. No explanations can affect the issue, no accounts of causes alter it. These are no more than the opinions people put forward in order to exercise their ingenuity in words without meaning on cases that cannot be solved, on happenings for which there is no solace. Even if we say that events are ordained from the beginning, we have not come to the end of the chain, and the matter is certainly not settled; nor does any knowledge of causes remove our disquiet. They found this, too, in Ginat's room: a deed of annulment, in which Ginat canceled the rights of the publishers to bring out his books, forbidding them to reprint his vocabulary (that is, the ninety-nine words of the Edo language), and his book of grammar (meaning the grammar of Edo), and his book of Enamite Hymns.

As usual, the dead man's orders were not carried out. On the contrary, his books are printed in increasing numbers, so that the world is already beginning to know his works, and especially the Enamite Hymns with their grace and beauty. While a great scholar lives those who choose to see his learning, see it; those who do not, see nothing there. But once he is dead, his soul shines out ever more brightly from his works, and anyone who is not blind, anyone who has the power to see, readily makes use of his light.

Annotations to "Edo and Enam"

In attempting to uncover the complexities of the kabbalistic sources woven throughout "Edo and Enam" (and the rest of Agnon's canon) the reader will find a very useful research tool in Elchanan Shilo, *HaKabbalah BeYetzirat Agnon* (Ramat Gan: Bar Ilan Univeristy Press, 2011).

Meshulam Tochner identifies the names Edo and Enam as echoing the roots of the Hebrew words *ye'ud* (destiny) and *ma'ayan* (source).

101. Riots of 1929 / Series of violent demonstrations and riots in August 1929 set off by a dispute between Muslims and Jews over access to Jerusalem's Western Wall, resulting in many Jewish deaths (most severely the massacre of 67 in Hebron) and widespread property damage. Agnon's home in Talpiot was marauded during these riots.

Agnon's library after the 1929 riots

103. Cadence of a woman's song / This is potentially a reference to the theory advanced by Shlomo Dov Goitein, who suggested that the Biblical Song of Songs was composed by a female court, but ascribed to Solomon, as was customary. He published this theory in the wake of his ethnographic studies on the Yemenite Jewish community and the Biblical cadences of its female poetic singers. Goitein (1900–85) was a distinguished historian, specializing in Jewish life under Medieval Islam, and was a close friend of Agnon. This topic is discussed, most recently, in Ilana Pardes, *Agnon's Moonstruck Lovers: The Song of Songs in Israeli Culture* (Seattle: University of Washington Press, 2013), pp. 60–65. Pardes' study focuses on the presence of the Song of Songs in the intertextual matrix of the two stories in this volume – "Betrothed" and "Edo and Enam".

S.D. Goitein

105. *Faust* / Faust, protagonist of a classic German legend, is a frustrated scholar whose pact with the Devil grants him unlimited knowledge in exchange for his soul. Goethe's *Faust* is an early 19th century play in two parts.

106. Solomon Ibn Gabirol / (c. 1021–1058) Among the greatest Hebrew poets and philosophers of Spanish Jewry. The legend of Ibn Gabirol's creating a female servant (à la legends of the Golem) is recorded in Joseph Solomon Delmedigo's 17th century work *Matzref LeHokhmah* (9b) and cited in Agnon's anthology *Sefer, Sofer ve-Sippur*, p. 244 (2000 edition).

Statue of Ibn Gabirol in Malaga, Spain

109. Mandate government / The British Mandate over Palestine administered civil affairs from 1920–1948.

109. Gederah / A town in central Israel.

111. Your happiness is where you are not / Closing line to Mordechai Zvi Maneh's 1884 poem *HaNoded* ("The Wanderer"). Maneh (1859–86) was a lyrical Hebrew poet of the First Aliyah period, who wrote longingly for the Land of Israel, although he died of tuberculosis before he could leave his native town of Radoshkovich (in today's Belarus). My thanks to Dr. Shuli Marom for help in identifying this line.

111. Gamzu / The character's name is likely a reference to the 1st century long-suffering Rabbi Nachum Ish-Gamzu, whose response to the many calamities which befell him (including blindness, similar to our character's loss of one eye), "*gam-zu le-tovah*" ("This, too, is for the best") became him moniker (Ta'anit 21a).

112. Gesenius' textbook / Wilhelm Gesenius (1786–1842), a German orientalist and Biblical critic, was the author of multiple lexicons and grammar books concerning Biblical Hebrew.

Wilhelm Gesenius

112. Twelve pounds / The Palestinian Pound (*lira*) was the currency in use during the British Mandate, linked in value to the British Pound Sterling, and then maintained in the early years of

One Palestine Pound

the State of Israel. Adjusted for inflation to 2011, twelve *lirot* would have been worth about $900.

113. Going to the south... / Ecclesiastes 1:6.

114. Seven locks... seven keys / Likely based on idea of seven keys to the seven gates of the Temple courtyard; Tosefta Shekalim 2:15.

114. *Yiddal, yiddal, yiddal, vah, pah, mah* / The enigmatic lyrics of Gemulah's song have remained a mystery for critics of this story. Tochner interprets the "*Yiddal*" song as a acronymic hint to the concluding phrase in Song of Songs 4:16: "Awake, O north wind, and come, O south wind; blow upon my garden, that the spices thereof may flow out; *let my beloved come to his garden (Yavo Dodi Le-gano) and eat his sweet fruit (Ve-yokhal Peri Megadav)* – with the word for "garden" ("*gano*") echoing the meaning and root of the name Dr. Ginat.

114. Gemulah / Cf. Rosh Hashanah 26a, in which R. Akiva interprets the word "*gemulah*" as connoting a woman "separated from her husband". The kabbalistic-allegorical interpretation of the story points out the resonance between Gemulah and "*gemilut hessed*" (lit. performance of acts of kindness) which is kabbalistically identified by Tikkunei Zohar (114b) with the *Shekhinah* (God's divine presence).

115. Dr. Rechnitz / The protagonist of Agnon's novella "Betrothed", which opens this volume.

117. *Hakham* / Hebrew for Sage, as in a Rabbinic Sage, but here can also mean a scholar or academic.

118. Nature of man has changed / An idea advanced by the early medieval rabbis, but evidenced already in the Talmud.

118. All depends upon one's star / Mo'ed Katan 28a.

118. Our star makes us wise, or makes us rich / Shabbat 156a.

118. Ibn Ezra / R. Abraham Ibn Ezra (Spain, 1089–1164), was a preeminent medieval Biblical commentator, philosopher, grammarian,

and poet. The statement quoted here appears in the Commentary to Exodus 15:17.

118. The Lord hath made everything for His own sake / Proverbs 16:4.

119. Sing out to the Lord in praise / Psalms 147:7.

119. The heavens declare the glory of God… / Psalms 19:2.

119. This people that I have created… / Isaiah 43:21.

119. Letters of the word "heaven" equal numerically to those of "male and female" / According to the *gematriya* method of assigning numerical value to each letter, heaven (*shamayim*) and "male and female" (*zakhar u-nekevah*) both equal 390.

119. Children of Benjamin… daughters of Shiloh / As related in Judges 21, during the period following the battle in Gibeah, when the other Israelite tribes would not allow their daughters to marry sons of the tribe of Benjamin.

119. Temple would be built / The site of the Jerusalem Temple straddles the territory of the Tribe of Benjamin.

119. Amadia / Small, ancient Assyrian and Kurdish town in Iraqi Kurdistan. The town is built on the flat top of a mountain, formerly only accessible by a narrow stairway cut into the rock. Amadia was the birthplace of the 12th century false Messiah, David Alroy, who led a revolt against the city but was defeated and killed in the process, as related in Benjamin of Tudela's near contemporaneous travelogue.

Amadia

120. The case of a person who was passing behind the synagogue / Mishnah Rosh Hashanah 3:7.

120. And to Gad he said… / Genesis 33:20.

120. Gad, a troop shall overcome him… / Jacob's blessing to the tribe of Gad in Genesis 49:19.

120. Which they took up beyond the Jordan / The tribe of Gad was settled on the eastern banks of the River Jordan (see Numbers 32:1–5).

120. Aramaic Targum / An exegetical translation of the Bible into Aramaic by Onkelos (c. 35–120 CE). The comment appears at Genesis 49:19.

121. Jerusalem Targum / A later translation of the Bible into Aramaic of the Land of Israel, including many interpretive and homiletic passages woven into the translation.

121. Face of a lion… / Cf. Ezekiel 1:10 (the description of the Divine Chariot).

121. High praises of God… two-edged sword… / Cf. Psalms 149:6.

121. Daughters of Israel went out to dance / Cf. Mishnah Ta'anit 4:8.

122. *Kavanim* / As Gamzu explains, these are "a kind of flat cake which they bake on live coals," but commentators on the story have alternatively identified Gemulah's *kavanim* with the kabbalistic notion of *kavanot* (mystical intentions) or with some form of pagan practice.

123. I am looking at the vessel and not what it contains / Inversion of Mishnah Avot 4:20: "Said Rabbi Meir: Look not at the vessel, but at what it contains."

124. Unto three transgressions of Israel… / Amos 2:6.

124. No man of Israel passes through this world more than two or three times… Even go through a thousand cycles of life / The discussion about the limits to the number of reincarnations of the soul is based on Tikkunei Zohar 32 (76b) and in the 16th century *Sefer HaGilgulim* of R. Chaim Vital (chapter 4 at 7a).

124. He commanded it unto the thousandth generation / Psalms 105:8.

125. Georgian Quarter at the Damascus Gate / The Damascus gate is one of the main entrances to Jerusalem's Old City, at the northwestern side of the surrounding city walls. The Georgian Quarter, known in Hebrew as the Eshel Avraham neighborhood, lies immediately outside the gate and was

Orange sellers at Damascus Gate (1944)

founded by Jewish immigrants from the country of Georgia in the 1890s.

125. Garmisch / A Bavarian mountain resort town in southern Germany.

126. Minyan / A quorum of ten men necessary to recite parts of the communal prayers and public Torah reading.

127. *Gemeinschaft der Gerechten* / German for: Society of Justice.

Djemal Pasha

127. Gamal Pasha / Djemal Pasha (1872–1922), Ottoman military leader during World War I.

127. Earthquake / Major earthquake on July 11, 1927, centered in Jericho caused mass damage throughout Mandatory Palestine – including more than 130 deaths and 300 house collapses in Jerusalem alone. Agnon's home in the center of Jerusalem was damaged, after which he relocated to the Talpiot neighborhood (then a new suburb of southern Jerusalem), where he spent the rest of his life.

1927 earthquake, Old City of Jerusalem

129. Rabbi Shmuel Rosenberg / Rosenberg (1842–1919) was a prominent anti-Zionist leader, who served as rabbi from 1884 in the town of Innsdorf (or Unsdorf), which is known today as Huncovce, northern Slovakia.

131. Amrami / Amram was the father of Moses (Exodus 6:20).

132. To the place where a man is summoned… / Cf. Sukkah 53a.

132. I came once to a certain village… / The description of Gamzu's journeys have parallels in the travelogue of Yaakov HaLevi Saphir's *Even Sappir* (2 vols., 1866 and 1874), who travelled to Yemen in search of the lost tribes. (This source was identified by Michal Oron, "Kabbalistic Symbols and Motifs in *Edo and Enam*" [in Hebrew] in *BaSeminar* [1977]). Agnon's copies of Saphir's books are still in the collection of the Agnon House library.

Yaakov Saphir (1859)

132. And He is merciful / Psalms 78:38; introductory verse to the weekday evening prayer, not generally recited on the Sabbath.

132. Nebuchadnezzar / Nebuchadnezzar II (c. 634–562 BCE), king of the Babylonian Empire, responsible for the destruction of

the First Temple in Jerusalem, and forced exile of the Jewish tribes.

132. The young men carried a grinding mill / Lamentations 5:13 and Midrash Eikhah Rabbati 5:14. The motif of the stones "flying on high like wings" is present in Midrash Shir HaShirim 1:4.

133. He weakened my strength on the way / Psalms 102:24.

133. From Bashan I shall bring… / Psalms 68:23.

134. Happy is the people… / Psalms 144:15.

134. The Lord will reign / Exodus 15:18.

135. Rabbi Dosa… *El Adon* / Early liturgical poem recited as part of the Sabbath morning service, ascribed here to Rabbi Dosa, whose name appears in acrostic.

135. Rabbi Adiel, who composed the hymn, "This people which Thou didst create…" / This does not appear to be an actual hymn, but likely a reference to Adiel Amzeh, the protagonist of Agnon's novella *Ad 'Olam* ("Forevermore"); his last name, Amzeh ("this people"), being a reference to Isaiah 43:21.

139. Rabbi Alshikh… whether a man is judged every day / R. Moshe Alshikh (1508–93, Safed) was a prominent kabbalist and Bible commentator. The debate about daily vs. yearly judgment appears in Rosh Hashanah 16a.

140. *Concise Shulhan Arukh* / *Kitzur Shulhan Arukh*, guide to practical *halakhah* by Rabbi Shlomo Ganzfried (1804–86, Hungary).

140. Judah Halevi / Spanish Jewish physician and philosopher (c. 1075–1141), considered one of the greatest Hebrew poets, both for his religious and secular poems, many of which appear in present-day liturgy. His greatest philosophical work was *The Kuzari*.

140. Luzzato / Samuel David Luzzatto (1800–65) was an Italian Jewish scholar, poet, and a member of the *Wissenschaft des Judentums* movement.

S.D. Luzzato

144. He who knows his place / Cf. Avot 6:6.

146. And a word was secretly brought to me… / Job 4:12.

148. Sukkah / An outdoor booth or hut for the seven-day Sukkot festival, see Leviticus 23:42.

148. The palm of a hand reached out / Cf. Ta'anit 29a, description of the metaphorical Divine hand reaching out to grab the Temple keys as it burned – a scene similarly played out on a rooftop.

150. The law of Moses and of Israel / From the traditional formula of the Jewish marriage vow.

150. The moon went her way... / Cf. Yerushalmi Rosh Hashanah 1:4 (58a).

150. Samaritan / Descendants of the sect of converts (described in Kings II 17:24), whose conversion to Judaism was questioned then subsequently rejected by Rabbinic Judaism. Fewer than 1,000 Samaritans remain in Israel today.

150. Giv'at Shaul / Neighborhood at the western entrance to Jerusalem, established in 1906.

150. Gvilan / *Gvil* is the Hebrew term for parchment.

150. Gagin / Rabbi Chaim Avraham Gagin (1787–1848) was a noted Jerusalem kabbalist who was responsible for saving the Samaritan community from a potentially fatal persecution at the hands of Ibrahim Pasha of Egypt in 1831. The dates of this Gagin cannot align with our story, but Agnon may be trying to work in some connection here.

151. Behold that which I have seen... / Ecclesiastes 5:17.

151. Behind the back of the world / Bava Batra 25a.

152. Going to the south, turning to the north, turning turning / Ecclesiastes 1:6.

155. Charity saves from death / Proverbs 10:2 and 11:4.

155. Mount of Olives / Site of an ancient Jewish cemetery to the east of the Old City of Jerusalem.

Mount of Olives funeral procession (c. 1900), with view of Old City walls

Agnon's Symbolic Masterpieces

W hen the two tales that comprise this volume were first published in translation, only months before S.Y. Agnon's receiving the 1966 Nobel Prize in Literature, only two other volumes of his were available in English. Those works, *The Bridal Canopy* and *In the Heart of the Seas,* are so intricately layered with the lore of Jewish tradition that they surely lay outside the imaginative grasp of most American readers. With the appearance of *Two Tales* nearly fifty years ago, readers were able to sample the more modernist phase of Agnon's varied yet deeply unified enterprise, coordinate products of his experiments in symbolic narrative during the 1940s and '50s. That this volume's two long stories appeared at the moment that the Swedish Academy helped bring world attention to a Hebrew writer in Israel (still the only such decorated Israeli author), helped readers of Agnon in English more fully appreciate the range and variety of his canon.

My own assessment of these stories, both when they appeared and now upon reexamination a half century later, can be stated quite simply: they seem to me to be among the more remarkable short symbolic fictions written anywhere during the twentieth century. In both, the element of storytelling is finely managed, an artful leisure-liness alternating with the evocative narration of tensely dramatic moments. As a result, one can be intrigued by the stories without having altogether fathomed them, but an awareness of their symbolic dimensions does a great deal to illuminate the nature of Agnon's art, and so I would like to offer here some brief commentary on the symbolism of "Betrothed" and "Edo and Enam" in the hope it will help establish a useful perspective for thinking about these *Two Tales*.

The two stories appear to be striking contrasts to one another but in fact they are perfect complements – two different faces of the same profound spiritual malaise. "Betrothed," the first of the stories, is set in Jaffa early in the twentieth century: it seems to be a more or less realistic tale (though the realism is breached at points), with seemingly romantic trappings, about two childhood friends who take a vow of eternal love in a Viennese garden and come to fulfill their pledge years later on the sands of the Mediterranean in the Land of Israel.

On the other hand, the events of "Edo and Enam," which takes place in Jerusalem after the Second World War, call attention repeat-edly, even bizarrely, to their own status as imaginative inventions: the names in the title refer to two supposed ancient cultures, in the dis-covery of which the lives of the principal characters are implicated; magic charms and mystic lore play central roles in the story; and, as if to remind us that the world of this tale is founded in the privacies of its author's imagination, Agnon assigns all the characters, and even most of the places mentioned, names beginning with either *'ayin* or *gimmel*, the first two letters of his own last name.

In all these differences, the two stories merely offer alternative symbolic images and alternative modes of fiction for the same general phenomenon – an attempted and failed relationship with the past. In "Betrothed" it is a personal past that implies a large cultural past as well, in "Edo and Enam" a cultural past that consumes the lives of individuals.

Gideon Ginat, the enigmatic figure to whom all the main char-acters of "Edo and Enam" are drawn, is a scholar who has unearthed the Enamite Hymns, in which one can hear "the reverberation of a primeval song passed on from the first hour of history through endless generations." Jacob Rechnitz, the protagonist of "Betrothed," might appear to pursue a more prosaic line of scientific research as a marine biologist, an investigator of seaweed, but we are reminded of Ginat upon learning that Rechnitz's passion for the plants of the sea began when he heard the surge of the ancient deep in the poetry of Homer and had a vision of the sea as the place "where the earliest ancestors of man had their dwelling."

In both cases, moreover, the attraction of the primeval past is, in a peculiar way, erotic. The key to the enigma of prehistory reaches Ginat through the agency of a hauntingly beautiful woman named Gemulah, the only daughter of a Jewish chieftain whose people has been forgotten in a hinterland of geography and time. Jacob Rechnitz often thinks of the sea in the language of human passion: "My orchard, my vineyard, he would say lovingly," echoing a metaphor of the Biblical Song of Songs for woman's sexual treasure.

His relationship with Shoshanah Ehrlich, the girl to whom he had pledged himself as a child, reproduces on a personal scale his relationship with the sea. Their ceremony of betrothal had taken place by a luxuriant pond in Shoshanah's garden and at one point Rechnitz imagines this as the source of his fascination with underwater flora. Through the distorting prism of dream memory, he sees Shoshanah emerging from the garden-pond "covered with wet seaweed like a mermaid, the water streaming from her hair."

The garden of childhood suggests the personal Eden of earliest life we all experience and irrevocably lose. In his attachment to Shoshanah Ehrlich, Rechnitz unconsciously seeks to recapture a pristine period of simple joy in his own life, just as in his attachment to the sea he is moved by the recollection of an earlier, more vital period in the life of humankind. Ironically, he becomes a kind of captive both to his beloved sea and to his betrothed Shoshanah.

The bewitching, deceptive, and finally lethal allure of the remote past is embodied in both stories in the symbol of the moon. Gemulah is a somnambulist, or "moonstruck," as the Hebrew, *saharonit*, suggests – fated whenever the full moon shines to go wandering over the rooftops, from Gabriel Gamzu, the husband of her unconsummated marriage, to Gideon Ginat, the man she strangely loves.

Shoshanah Ehrlich is another kind of somnambulist, stricken with an uncanny sleeping sickness, who in a more naturalistic way also seems under the fascination of the moon. The sea with which she is linked in Rechnitz's mind is in turn governed by the moon, and not only in the movement of its tides: when Rechnitz first conjures up its primordial presence upon reading Homer, "the moon hovered over the face of the waters, cool and sweet and terrible."

In Genesis, we remember, it is the spirit of God that hovers over the face of the waters, but the world of both these stories is dominated by a kind of erotic lunar demiurge whose creation, unlike God's, has bottomless abysses, dizzying confusions of heights and depths, and no eternally appointed boundary between sea and land. The charmed leaves brought back by Gemulah's father from a mountain cave, with their cryptic lines that look for a moment like the silver strands of the moon, belong to the same ambiguous sphere as Rechnitz's seaweed hauled up from the bottom of the Mediterranean.

Agnon makes the identification explicit in Gabriel Gamzu's account of the leaves: "As I stood gazing, the colors…changed into the tints of seaweeds drawn from the depths, such weeds as Dr. Rechnitz drew up from the sea near Jaffa." At the beginning of the climactic scene in "Betrothed," the moon, in a single brief sentence, is simultaneously connected with sky and sea, frantic restlessness, poignant but maddened desire: "Up above, and under the surface of the sea, the moon raced like a frenzied girl."

The terminus in both stories for the moon as a symbol of spellbound love is death. "I shall sing the song of the Grofit, and then we shall die," Gemulah tells Ginat, and their relationship is indeed consummated in death. Shoshanah, who is the focal point of the terrible ennui that pursues most of the principals in "Betrothed," longs for death, for the eternity of blissful extinction of an Egyptian mummy, just as Rechnitz associates her image with that of her dead mother, and the flowers that bind them both to the garden of their childhood with the flowers piled high on Frau Ehrlich's hearse.

At the end of the story, when seven girls race on the beach for the prize of Jacob Rechnitz, the starting point is the Hotel Semiramis and the goal they run toward is an old Muslim cemetery. This is the course of both stories – from Semiramis, the queen who is a burning image of antiquity's erotic splendor, to a graveyard, from eros to thanatos, love to death.

Such symbolic patterns, which are a good deal more elaborate than this brief account can indicate, are cunningly contrived by Agnon, but what serves as a fuller measure of his stature as a writer is the profound correspondence of the symbols to the distinctive spiritual conditions of modern people.

A ubiquitous emptiness gnaws at the heart of the characters in both these stories: in "Betrothed" it finds expression in a sick girl, a nightmarish parrot screaming curses in German, an old man endlessly smoking cigars and telling pointless stories; in "Edo and Enam" its chief embodiment is a universal state of homelessness, a world where everyone fears for the roof over his head and keeps moving uneasily from place to place. People in both tales are unable to be with themselves in peace and unwilling to face squarely the world they inhabit.

The late Israeli critic, and a pioneer of Agnon studies, Baruch Kurzweil (whose analysis of these stories is at some points brilliant, at others misleading, too) aptly observed that the vogue of the archaic in modern culture – certainly as Agnon sees it – is a symptom of spiritual bankruptcy, an illusory attempt at renewal which is but a step in a process of decay.

We can readily apply Kurzweil's generalization to the erotic elements of both stories: the remotest past, appearing to possess vitality, intensity, a capacity for simple abandon – all qualities our own lives often seem to lack – beckons with the magic of female seductiveness. But because so much history intervenes between it and us, any attempt to unite with it, from Nietzsche and James George Frazer's *The Golden Bough* (a comparative study of magical and religious beliefs) to the cult of archeology and the Israeli "Canaanite" movement (both fashionable forces when Agnon composed these tales in the 1940s), is a mockery of true union, a mating of flesh with ashes, distracted living spirit with unknowable spectral memory.

At one point early in "Edo and Enam," someone half-jokingly conjectures that Dr. Ginat might well be sitting in his room writing a third part to *Faust*. From one point of view, this is really what *Two*

Tales is. Faust, so given to confounding the passions of the spirit with the passions of the flesh, possesses an earthly beauty then unwittingly destroys her in the first part of Goethe's poem, while in the second part he descends into classical antiquity to possess ideal beauty in Helen, who finally eludes him.

Agnon's modern Fausts, in different ways, descend still lower in their quests, themselves possessed by the alien and impenetrable beauty of a primordial age whose attainment means extinction, a point where beginning and end are one. This is by no means the whole of Agnon's vision of past and present, but it is a significant, and deeply troubling, aspect of his inner world and ours, and in these two stories he has given this haunted sense of reality the solidity of perfectly wrought language and symbol and imagined act.

Robert Alter is Emeritus Professor of Hebrew and Comparative Literature at the University of California, Berkeley. He has written extensively on modern Hebrew literature and on the Bible as well as on the European and American novel.

About the Author

S.Y. Agnon (1888–1970) was the central figure of modern Hebrew literature, and the 1966 Nobel Prize laureate for his body of writing. Born in the Galician town of Buczacz (in today's western Ukraine), as Shmuel Yosef Czaczkes, he arrived in 1908 in Jaffa, Ottoman Palestine, where he adopted the penname Agnon and began a meteoric rise as a young writer. Between the years 1912 and 1924 he spent an extended sojourn in Germany, where he married and had two children, and came under the patronage of Shlomo Zalman Schocken and his publishing house, allowing Agnon to dedicate himself completely to his craft. After a house fire in 1924 destroyed his library and the manuscripts of unpublished writings, he returned to Jerusalem where he lived for the remainder of his life. His works deal with the conflict between traditional Jewish life and language and the modern world, and constitute a distillation of millennia of Jewish writing – from the Bible through the Rabbinic codes to Hasidic storytelling – recast into the mold of modern literature.

About the Translator and Editor

Walter Lever (translator) was born in London and arrived in Jerusalem in 1947 to teach English Literature at the Hebrew University, where he became a significant translator of Hebrew literature to English. Later he returned to serve as a lecturer at Durham University in England, and published a memoir of his early days in Israel entitled *Jerusalem is Called Liberty*.

Jeffrey Saks is the Series Editor of The S.Y. Agnon Library at The Toby Press, and lectures regularly at the Agnon House in Jerusalem. He is the founding director of ATID – The Academy for Torah Initiatives and Directions in Jewish Education and its WebYeshiva.org program.

The fonts used in this book are from the Garamond family.